The
Seamless
Universe

For Mike & Hoff in seamless friendship

The
Seamless
Universe

Battle Lines Are Drawn

A Contemporary Fantasy

By

KATHLEEN RIPLEY LEO

ISBN: 1499230877
ISBN 13: 9781499230871
Library of Congress Control Number: 2014907647
CreateSpace Independent Publishing Platform
North Charleston, South Carolina

Dedicated to:
J ANE A NN R IPLEY

from whom our family learned to stretch our wings, and that
anything is possible

PART ONE
The Feud

~ Chapter 1 ~

"Colt," Bret caught his brother's attention, incredulity causing a grimace to shadow his handsome features. "Where are all the raptors?"

A shrug. "Don't ask for trouble. Let's just do our job and get out of here."

Bret and Colt along with four others of their Tureg fey anxiously searched the blue sky for signs of condors. Or hawks, or fish eagles. Any kind of raptor on the hunt for a tasty mouthful of fey.

The Tureg fey were as small as yellow jacket hornets and hardly visible suspended in flight five inches above the oily ocean surface. They were far away from any land mass. Birds of prey had sharp eyes, though. The oil was a heavy mirror on the surface of the ocean and reflected the sky and the clouds. The Tureg could see themselves in it, as well as watch for flying predators. They knew that to touch this mirror was to come away slicked over with a heavy gloss, suffocating to the skin, just as it would be for the underwater flora and fauna if they couldn't fix this. What a dirty mission.

They were here to take care of this problem, but they had to keep safe, too. Their bright wings shone blue green. That was indeed colorful, just like the languid swirl of color that slowly rose above their heads. Handsome, and dangerous.

"Will you stop that!" Colt cast a frown toward Bret.

"What are you talking about?" Bret's surprised expression now intensified his bright good looks. His dark eyebrows lifted dramatically, contrasting with his light hair and hazel eyes.

"You kicked my left wing – again."

"I did not."

"Yes, you did!"

"Hey, get out of my way!"

The other Tureg were used to this bickering and ignored the brothers. All six of the fey morphed larger so their larger wings could generate a stronger wind to direct the clogging murky oil into a manageable blob. Predators could hide in the swells, making the need for a posted sentry mandatory. Zac did that duty today, but they all were on the lookout. Bret and Colt had heard the words, Dive, Dive, many times before but not out here. So far. Bret's ingrained raptor sensor was in overdrive. Even seagulls could be a problem for the fey.

This particular disaster had been put into motion millennia ago. Deep wells of trapped primeval oil had found a way to seep up through the ocean crust heaving with its full strength until a fissure cracked wide open and violent. The flood of viscous crude covered a huge ocean surface nearly horizon to horizon. And more was still to spew. Yet it was a flood that would be contained once the rock and detritus deep on the ocean floor were manipulated to close up. The Tureg could handle that.

The seamless universe gave, and the seamless universe took away. How Bret wished that all such problems in the garden could be so easily solved. Bret and Colt along with Jarret and Brant made their way down through the water while Zac and Vincent began the surface task of oil containment. Along the way they encountered few sea creatures among the statuesque columns of ocean depth chimney rock and towering seaweed. Good, they'd be well advised to avoid this part of the endless sea for the time being. It was deep here, nearly two miles down, but it wasn't hard to spot the enormous gush of oil. Their Tureg healing power was all they needed to manipulate the gusher to close up. Slowly the vast hole became smaller and smaller. The gush became a trickle. Colt told Bret he'd stay with Jarret and Brant until it was finished.

Half the crisis was solved, and now the surface of the ocean needed attention. Bret wound his way back to the air, and surveyed what Zac and Vincent had already accomplished. The few white shreddy clouds overhead speckled a brilliant cerulean sky. Just the color Tureg prized and it was a reminder that their mission was to keep the entire garden safe. Not only the water mass, but the land mass, too. So many missions, too little time to do it all. Back to the task at hand.

Taking positions equi-distant around the edges of the spill, the three Tureg batted their hyper-charged wings against the spreading oil until it shrank down to a more manageable blob. Bret conferred with Zac and together they flew off to awaken beetles hibernating in the tidal flats' sloggy sand and water, faraway at the edge of the land mass. Bret and Zac led them like a crusading navy to the oil. The chemistry in their bodies provided a filtering system that cleansed the water surface. The Tureg looked on in amazement as dark little iridescent beetles chomped and churned. Slowly the oily sludge thinned until there were only slight blooms of oil here and there that reflected rainbows, as they do in oil slicks on roads. The beetles swarmed back into hibernation to await the next fey call.

"That looks as good as it's going to get. Pretty much like the last time we were here. Still, I wonder where the raptors are?" asked Zac. Zac was Bret's best friend, and together they looked out for each other out in the vast garden.

"I don't know, but like Colt said, let's not ask for trouble."

One rift in the precarious ecology of the garden was healed. From the very beginning of the seamless universe Tureg mission was to rectify the problems the act of creation had produced in the garden. Immense pressures in the ocean crust and in the land erupted now and then into earthquakes, into tsunamis, into all kinds of trouble. Many slight manipulations were needed like this one, day in and day out.

It was clear they had done all they could do, and it really did look pretty good. Colt and his taskforce could handle the ocean floor while the two other Tureg flew toward home. Bret decided that since one job was finished he'd go off and take care of another mission, a rescue of a totally different nature.

Bret left the endless sea and approached land. He watched for condors and vultures. The sky was clear. Ever since he'd grown from a changeling into full grown fey his raptor sensor worked very well. His fey father Selat said his was the best he'd ever known about. His mother Sulpicett too was amazed at her son's ability. It was an exceptional gift from the original creative spirit.

As Bret flew through the countryside he thanked the seamless universe for his strong wings. Like others in the Tureg they were composed of antrei, the glass-like panes similar to a cathedral's rose point window. It was natural in the Tureg fey for coloration to run to different shades of blue and green. Mixed in subtly when the sun shone on him were flashes of red and yellow, spikes of warm coloration that subtly balanced out the cool color spectrum. He reverted to his small yellow jacket size and flew the great distance quickly.

The red brick hospital lay sprawled before him with ambulances parked close in on the west side parking lot. He'd been here before. To the east, Bret noticed the fast running river with large schools of fish heading upstream. He could tell it was a strong salmon run, although he was not here to note the fauna balances. Otherwise he'd have to go in search of brown bears. Predator-prey mission. So many missions, so little time to do it all. Bret headed for the hospital.

Once inside he flew down the familiar wide white halls in his even smaller sized no-see-um wisp form and looked for the maternity ward. A mix of emotions began to stir as he contemplated the scenes that awaited him. On one hand, he felt clear satisfaction that ephemeral rescue was the Tureg gift to people. On the other hand, foreboding because of the heightened emotions in maternity wards, still worse in the sub-basements of hospitals where those bereft of life were taken. Tureg were able to cope with the surge of human grief that the death of an infant caused. For grieving parents still at the hospital it was very difficult. Live-born infants could look forward to a long life on the vast and generous human scale. The doors to the happy families were open, rooms fragrant with flowers, laughter and song springing in the air. He spotted a closed door that had a picture of a rose on it. This was a sign there were grieving people inside. He took a deep breath and looked back at the hallway he'd just flown.

Bret spotted the cleaning cart a bit further down the hall. That's it! He became a human by instantaneous morphing, this time a cleaning man with his supplies. He didn't have to do that, but it was easier than waiting for someone to open the door. Depending on available props he could transform himself into any camouflage. He was glad for this one since he could go about his business with little notice. He opened the door, walked in and softly said he was going to pick up the trash from the few containers in the room.

It was a large birthing room with the mother in a bed in the middle. The air surrounding the bed was a palpable veil of pale yellow. Right away he saw this might be a good day for the fey, while a tragedy for the people. Bret knew that the two parents cradling their infants did not see the faint trace of red, blue and yellow colors slowly swirling above the small heads. How could they know that from their own shoulders spiraled the colors of grayish green entwined with rose pink? The parents would not feel the soft touch of spring breezes he felt on his face. These signs meant that these infants, with their souls safely back with the original creative spirit, could have a chance at an existence as a changeling. Ephemeral hopes were strong.

Swirling primary colors meant that the ephemerals were as vigorous as any he'd rescued. Not only that. Also streaming in the color swirls were shifting numerals that switched from exquisite equations totaling the sum of the seamless universe to simple sums. He knew that only he in the room could hear the slight buzzing sound emanating from the infants. Colors, numbers, and the sense of touch were within his Tureg perception. The additional buzzing confirmed it was exactly what he looked for in his rounds at hospital after hospital.

He waited back in a corner, picking up things now and then, eyes downward, giving the family their privacy. A few quiet nurses came in and out speaking softly to the mother who lay on the bed with her small daughter in her arms and a basket at her side. The basket looked like a small cradle and the baby girl looked asleep in her tiny pink hat, her body covered by a crocheted blanket. Mother's arms surrounded her child, gently holding her, gazing with love. Grandparents sat in their nearby chairs comforting as best they could with their presence. Their faces were resigned and stoic.

The father sat at the edge of the bed and rocked his other daughter in his arms, singing to her, talking to her. She was covered in a pink blanket, she had her own crocheted hat, and her basket lay on the counter behind him. The room contained large pieces of equipment. On the walls were gold-framed pictures of flowers and babies held by smiling moms and dads. For these people they must have been sad reminders of their loss.

How many times had Bret witnessed this? The infants had passed through rigor mortis and the family could play with their flexible fingers remarking how the fingers are long, like mom's, perhaps she will play the piano. The eyebrows are arched like dad's, wouldn't she be a clear thinker. Parents would speak in past tense, present tense, mixing it up with the future, sweetly chattering to their babies in an attempt to provide a lifetime of wisdom into the few days allotted them to hold their small bodies.

Bret knew their grief would encompass a time and parceling out of its own. The hospital kept the infants so parents could call for them until they were ready to let them go. This was a hospital policy aimed at helping parents grieve. Sometimes it was days or even a week that they wanted to hold them before the final goodbye. Either way, the heavy pale yellow veil of sorrow hung on the shoulders of any bereaved family for the rest of their lives. It grew less heavy as time healed small parts of this bitter wound.

If they only knew, Bret thought, it might give them some comfort. Time and again the fey had affirmed not to reveal the gift the original creative spirit had given the seamless universe. These children were not destined for humanity and all of its joys. As changelings, though, they would take on another purpose.

Bret stayed in the back of the room and waited. He made a mental note and would look in on the parents once he transported the ephemerals to the Tureg nursery. And after the mother and father had returned to their home in the garden, as is the way of the seamless universe.

It was time. The mother's face twisted, tears trailed down from her beautiful blue eyes, and she put her daughter into the basket and let the nurse take her away. The father did the same with their other daughter. Both mother and father dropped into each other's arms.

The nurse walked away. She carried the two baskets easily since they were so small. Bret left to follow the nurse as she traversed hall after hall down elevators to the sub-basement floor. Along the way he quickly stepped into a closet, stored the cleaning cart, morphed into his tiny fey form and caught up to the nurse. Finally, they arrived at the cold room. The nurse placed the infants on a gurney and left. Now there was a vigorous swirl of blue, yellow and scarlet hanging above each of them, a very strong showing. The small jewels of intensity that were their ephemerals were firmly intact. They promised to make outstanding changelings.

Normally he rescued one at a time because any ephemerals left behind would make their way back to the original creative spirit, just like the soul had. The Tureg could not possibly rescue all ephemerals but these two both exhibited such intense colorations he decided not to separate them. The choice was up to him. The parents would never know. They'd have their infants to mourn and the fey would have their ephemerals. There were two beds waiting in the Tureg nursery deep in the cavern underneath the blue indigo bush by the sea.

Milkweed pod beds stood waiting to bestow ephemerals with life again, purposeful in the flash of color known as fey.

~ Chapter 2 ~

Bret laid each ephemeral in the arms of two Tureg nursery attendants who then slipped them into milkweed pods lined with silky prairie smoke tendrils. The fluttery ends waved back and forth in the air. Jondett, the head of the Tureg nursery looked on with approval and he was glad of her warm smile. He began to feel a silk scarf rubbing his cheek and a comforting caress of a hand through his hair. That was because of Jondett, no doubt about it.

Nothing was there, there was no hand giving him a caress. These sensations were part and parcel of being a Tureg. If he was doing something worthwhile, the physical reality felt gentle. If there was a problem, the invisible but very real sensation of a slap could leave a pretty good-sized bruise. Jondett was his sweet reminder of good things waiting for him in their future.

As he watched, Jondett beamed at him while she and her staff attended to the ephemerals. She was wearing a light blue robe, whose diaphanous fabric glistened with flakes of mica. Her long dark hair twitched at their ends as she bustled about. As transfixed as he was, he tried not to stare.

The prairie smoke tendrils that lined the milkweed pods were the first step, and they were carefully gathered in early spring from the land of the garden. The garden provided more than they needed, thank the seamless universe. A nursery should never be without prairie smoke tendrils.

What they didn't have enough of, what actually caused the final transformation, were Candela antrei. All Tureg felt an acute sadness at the waywardness of the seamless universe. The Tureg were not alone in the garden. Everyone knew about the Candela fey, the estranged Candela fey. They lived in a cavern deep within the prairie, far from the Tureg whose cavern was by the sea.

Not that Candela fey wings were much different in appearance than the Tureg's. All fey had colorful glowing wings. But the Candela's antrei were precious indeed. All Tureg wondered what was embedded in them. It had to be an intriguing combination of sensations: color, numbers, sound, taste, touch, and only the seamless universe knew what else. It was Candela antrei, and only theirs, that transformed ephemerals into changelings. Candela antrei shone with warm colors—reds, yellows, and oranges. Maybe that had something to do with it. No one really knew. The Tureg were mystified, and grudgingly acknowledged that the seamless universe and the original creative spirit must have known what they were doing.

Of all of Tureg missions, nursery care was highly sought. The nursery took up a large airy segment of the cavern. It was staffed with those who'd been well trained to care for ephemerals. It was always a joy to visit the Tureg nursery. Yet for Bret, it was Jondett with her beaming smile and twitching hair that made the nursery so beguiling. Jondett and he had been changelings at the same time, and trained together. Bret hoped that one day they would pair. He also hoped he was worthy and knew that she was.

His attention was drawn back to the milkweed pods where he saw the prairie smoke tendrils give a last languorous wave in the air before they finally settled down around each of the glowing bundles. Jondett and her two attendants had been hovering near the pods in a type of dance that mimicked the waving of the tendrils. The next step was to eventually surround a tendril-embraced ephemeral with a Candela antreus.

"I can't believe how large these ephemerals are," said Jondett, shaking her long dark hair back away from her face. "I've not seen such strong ones in a very long time. We better not wait. They'll burn out if we don't give them an antreus right now. Ouch!"

"Oh sorry, Jondett, I'm so clumsy."

"You know, the other guys don't step on my wings! Zac never does, Brant, either. What's wrong with you?"

"I said I was sorry."

"Bret, you stepped on my wing. You have to watch where you're going. Someday, buster, that'll get you in big hot water, big time." But the smile on her face told him he wasn't, at least not yet.

As to the antrei, it was an enduring problem. The biggest trouble facing the Tureg was not the oil spills on the ocean, or continental plate shifting, or even wildfires and increased predators. Those were bad enough. The problem was that the Candela had been withholding their antrei and by doing that they were putting the nursery in dire peril. Some in the Tureg attributed this to a feud of some nature that had been going on for such a long time no one was sure of its origin. The number of Candela antrei gathered for the nursery were limited to what the Tureg could find in the garden after they sloughed off and fell from Candela wings.

Sometimes Tureg came across a Candela and harvested antrei ready to fall off. Of course, that was risky in that the Tureg did not want to harm a Candela. Well, at least most of the Tureg thought that way. Why in the garden did the Candela refuse their antrei was the constant question. How could they be so selfish, so unaware? Especially since it was the Tureg that provided them with their own changelings...in secret, of course.

Soon after the ephemeral transformation was complete, it could be determined which changelings were Tureg and which were Candela. There was no way to tell ahead of time, or to interfere. Complicating everything was the fact that transformations could take place relatively quickly, or it might take a very long time. Each ephemeral was a unique individual.

Tureg changelings were given to waiting pairs deemed worthy to be parents. Candela changelings were brought to the sweet grass field and left for the Candela to find. That had been the way for a very long time.

Bret sighed as he watched Jondett open the large box encrusted with coquille shells and sand dollars where the antrei were stored. He knew he'd have to go out into the garden very soon, the box was woefully depleted. That was a mission for later. Talandat, their Regent, would mention it no doubt at next Assembly. It seemed that for as long as Bret could remember, the lack of antrei had been a subject for discussion at Assembly.

Jondett reached into the box. It contained only a few glowing wing partitions. "It's lucky that Zac brought some in just a few days ago." Bret noted with some irritation that Jondett smiled as she mentioned Zac's name.

Jondett took two antrei from the box and placed one on top of each of the tendril-laced ephemerals. With her quick fingers she efficiently tucked in and under the glowing bundles. Warm and cool colors began to coalesce in the swirls above the milkweed pods, a happy sight for all. Hazy numerals streamed, and a slight buzzing sound was heard. All of this was normal. Both Bret and Jondett looked down on the two pods tenderly. Perhaps both would one day be theirs to raise once the two of them were paired. Bret pointedly studied Jondett and hoped they were as well matched as he imagined.

Jondett turned to him and asked, "Will you tell me why you rescued both?" Her look was so sweet.

Bret waved his wings over their heads and spiraled bluish green and purple red. He felt smooth cashmere soft as the silky underside of lambs' ears. He smiled as he said, "I was only going to take one since they are fraternal twins. Then I saw that the original parents were so resolute in their love that they also spiraled gray and rose. Don't see that too often. Even the grandparents in the room were streaking color. I could tell that both are worthy."

The wisdom of his statement could not be denied. Tureg charged with rescue mission made the decision.

"I'll see you after Assembly later on this evening. Are you going?" Bret looked at Jondett with more than a question in his expression.

"No, my shift is very long today."

"I think I'll say hello to my parents and then go out to find antrei." With that, and several shy smiles at each other, Bret left the nursery in the caring hands of Jondett and her capable staff.

Bret moved into the main cavern. In the middle of the bright airy space was a chair fashioned from knobbed roots. This was where Talandat, Regent of the Tureg, sat during Assembly. Next to it was the knobby root table for the Tureg council members. The cavern was lined with row upon row of balconies; these were the Tureg living compartments. There were about twenty individual Tureg families for the time being. That represented eighty or so members in the community.

Swirling up and down in the main cavern were streams of translucent numerals and colors marking the paths that traced on up to individual balconies. Color and numbers and light, like translucent banners. Perpetually lit spheres suspended from the high ceiling, right next to replicas of star constellations. These reminded Tureg that the original creative spirit had gifted the seamless universe with this garden, and with fey when the first child laughed. The laughter broke apart into star-sprung sparks, and each became a faery.

Bret flew following a blue path speckled with vague, interwoven equations on over to the familiar light green path and soon arrived at his parents' household.

His father Selat sat at the table tinkering with his latest invention, and his mother Sulpicett was pouring glasses of dandelion tonic for their late afternoon repast. He noticed his brother Colt wasn't back yet from fixing the ocean disaster, but younger sister Margaret was sitting on the floor playing with her witch hazel rods. It looked, happily, like her changeling status was soon to be elevated to young adult Tureg. Her training would be enhanced and her mission would become apparent. No doubt a pairing would be in her near future. Bret wondered how many of his friends had begun to notice his sister. His eyes narrowed – they'd better be worthy.

Sulpicett said to her daughter, "One day you can use those rods to help a human find water in the desert. Witch hazel is an excellent fey tool."

"I know, mom, they told us that in class," Margaret looked at her mom with an aggrieved expression on her face, her eyes rolling. For young Tureg, adolescence was such a pain. Bret commiserated with her. It wasn't too long ago that he was in her place.

"Well, it's a mom's job to tell you!"

"Son, it's good to have you back. How did the ephemeral run go?" Selat was a celebrated rescuer and had trained his son well. Before he retired he'd provided some of the brightest ephemerals. Now Selat worked exclusively on observing and protecting the people.

Bret bent down to pat his pet starfish who had taken to clinging to the underside of the table. "I took two today, fraternal twin girls. Their colors were strong even though it had been several days. The original human parents were resolute in their love. And best of all when I gazed on the ephemerals I had the undeniable sensation of flying through clouds, through silky scarves, and diving down to the Sargasso Sea. Very powerful. I rescued both. I think something seamless in the universe happened today."

Bret heard his father sigh. "I hope you're also planning on going out to the garden to see what's there. Colt found very few antrei in the sweet grass field. How I wish their wings weren't the only ones that transformed. I wish ours could do the same."

His mother Sulpicett chimed in, "The Candela can't rescue the ephemerals, and we Tureg can't use our wings to transform them. What a garden."

"You can't blame that on us, mom," said Bret. "It's from the beginning of time itself."

Selat tried to twist a pliable lemon verbena branch around a sturdier one. "Hey, Bret, look at this. If I can figure out a better way to twine this together, one day we'll be able to dry spider silk more efficiently."

"Yeah, sure, dad. That's nice. Look, I think I'll go and see what's out there."

"Be careful, son. This goes without saying: don't harm a Candela any more than you have to. If one resists, you have to take their antrei, but be careful... whatever you do, don't hurt them, promise me."

"Dad, I've been at this a long time already!"

His mother shot him a worried look, too. "Son, we know you take care. But Talandat said they are looking very closely at how we harvest, especially recently. Something is going on, I don't know what it's all about. We don't want you punished."

Before he flew off to gather Candela antrei, Bret decided to look into the parents of the ephemerals he'd just rescued. There was always the possibility that he could do something unexpected to cheer them up, to help them see that happiness somewhere, some-how, was in their future.

Plus he especially wanted to see if they were all right, losing twins was a double blow. He shook his head at that. Any infant death was catastrophic. He knew that his own original human parents still grieved for him. He promised himself he'd make time to see how they were doing these days. Cheering up bereft parents was a mission he cherished.

He flew small as a wisp to the house. Outside he saw the mother cutting stems of coneflowers from a large clay urn. She started to walk back inside and he saw her look longingly at the gardenia plant.

That's it! He flew to the dark green bush, and felt the touch of a plushy gardenia petal on his cheek. That was all it took for two to appear in his hands. That, and visualizing the equation of one plus one. A simple sum. Bret grafted the two blooms together, like twins, onto one of the interior branches. It would look as if she'd just overlooked them the first time. He hid behind one of the glossy leaves and waited for her to come out again.

He could tell that she had been crying. That was the way of the seamless universe, it was so soon. The gift of life had been thwarted into shocking tragedy and became an unbidden rash that would chronically inflame her heart. Human grief was so sad to the Tureg. There were some people who could enjoy the bountiful fruits of creation all their time in the garden, and others who had to search for meaning in the seamless universe while coping with death, especially infant death.

She walked over to her gardenia and knelt down beside it. She stroked each leaf on the top branches and separated them. She gave a sharp intake of air. There in front of her were two perfect gardenia blooms embedded under a canopy of dark green, fragrant and clear white in color. She cupped the two together in the palms of her hands, carefully lifting the inner branch up so she could breathe in the fragrance. A small smile spread across her lovely face and her beautiful blue eyes filled again with tears. These tears were brilliant stars that this time reflected some tiny part of the healing gift.

Bret was satisfied with his efforts and flew off in search of antrei—one mission attended to, another one waiting.

~ Chapter 3 ~

Andrielle of the Candela fey grasped the first ledge rock at the bottom of the limestone wall. Rock over rock she made the difficult climb. Clammy dew and moss were no trouble nor did it bother her that filmy spider webs clung to her face. It was her wings—they hurt terribly. One of them, the right one, hung in tatters. The left one was not so bad but she really could not sustain flight. The Tureg had caught her, was going to beat her she was sure of it. She saw his raised arm. Then he suddenly flew away. No matter the reason, she had escaped. Then she tripped over hard scrabble roots and fell headlong into the dry gravel bed. It scraped her up good, not to mention that her wings beat against sharp gravel while she tried to right herself. That caused her wings, especially the right one to tatter. And on her first patrol. She could already hear the howls of laughter from her friends.

Yes, there's the chanterelle. She touched the under gill and gratefully was pulled in. She floated down into a light-filled cavern and heard the swirling splendid music all Candela heard. Even though the portal keeper Grandel knew her, he made her recite her identification: "High A is yellow quince," she intoned on a perfect pitch A flat. Sun-drenched yellow spiraled up from the good wing.

Music is color and taste, her fey. Andrielle had heard that a Tureg would have stated a number and a color. Their fey. Easy to tell them apart. Easy to keep them out.

Andrielle suddenly felt woozy and Grandel caught her before she sank down to the cavern floor. He called to another Candela and together they carried Andrielle through the right side corridor into a large well-lit cavern filled with groups of Candela fey. Wings fanned the air as music and color spiraled at will. Music was a comfort factor in her cavern and it cradled every thought the Candela had. Many faces turned to her as she was carried. Comforting arias trilled up and down the octaves. This felt safe, especially now. She was taken to her compartment on the high level of the cavern and set down on her bed. The silk from the butterfly plant pod soothed her as she settled in.

Her mother appeared at her side with screechy blats and blares that mirrored the desperate terror Andrielle knew her mother was feeling. This was no kind of soothing music.

"How did this happen to you? And on your first patrol?"

"Mother, the Tureg came at me out of nothing, from a flash of color. I was counting my steps like I was told to do. I thought I stopped on the eighth step. Maybe it wasn't. Maybe it was the eleventh."

"You forgot, Andrielle? It's like you painted a target on yourself. You're lucky you're still alive!" Discordant trills underscored with high G's and A's bounced off the walls.

"I forgot. I wore my anklet on my left instead of the right and I just lost count."

"You'll remember now." Gwen stood with her hands on her hips. Disapproval knitted her brow until her eyes filled with tears. A slow dirge in the key of E resonated throughout their living quarters. Finally an end of terror music.

Andrielle looked at the compartment window where the concerned faces of her friends Madison, Pamela, Carl, and Mitchell were crowding together. They had all been part of the same training class. Gwen threw her hands up as if to say, Fine! Andrielle beckoned them to come in.

"How could this happen! Are you ok?" Madison and Pamela's spirals were flaring. Carl and Mitchell looked as angry as Andrielle had ever seen a Candela. They were intoning the most disagreeable notes just like her mother had.

"Tell us who did this, we'll go after him!" Carl shouted.

Pamela spoke with an appalled look, "How do we know it's a 'him'? Tureg females are just as bad."

Gwen brought them up short, "Kids, your music is blaring and blatting, I can't hear myself think. Do you think that's good for Andrielle?"

"Why did this happen to me?" Andrielle was forlorn. Her friends would be making their first watch very soon, and she wanted to be a good role model for them. Guess not.

Gwen pushed Andrielle's four friends away, "Let me look at her—in peace!" Gwen carefully pulled the right wing back and forth, grimacing along with Andrielle for the pain this caused. "Looks like torn antrei in the right wing, and fractured nicotinic tissue. We've got to get you to the healer." Her mother was an elder in the Candela. She could diagnose, but not heal.

Andrielle's wings were one of the rare kind in her fey. No wonder the Tureg went after them. As her wings flashed, each antreus glowed with a smear of color, one bluish, one reddish, one yellowish and pink, each with a crystalline glow. There might have been forty or fifty antrei in her wings. She'd had full grown wings since her changeling days were over. Now she stood as tall as her next oldest sister. Andrielle was a young adult fey ready and primed to live up to Candela mission.

At first her wings had grown out of her shoulders as small short sprouts and hooked down into narrow points. Later they matured and migrated down to her waist growing into the two part wings they were now. The top halves were almost circular and stretched over her head, the bottom oblong halves reached to the floor. Both top and lower halves were edged with filmy lace-like fronds. At rest, her wings sumptuously swayed, much like the undersides of sand dollars, refracting over and over again the entire spectrum of color. They could move independently which caused symphonic music and four colors to spiral above her shoulders instead of the usual two or three. They were something to behold.

Madison came around the bed to stand beside Andrielle. Her smaller wings were different than Andrielle's in that even though they were made of two parts, Madison had an elongated oblong part on top, and a shortened oval one on the lower half. By contrast, Pamela had singular wings which came out of her body close to her shoulders, and hooked down. Each of hers was composed of a single glazed antreus and they blazed with constantly changing colors as Pamela flashed from one emotion to another. Carl and Mitchell's wings were alike, perhaps because they were ephemeral twin brothers, identical at their beginning. Like Pamela they too had one part wings that began near their waists and widened ever larger so that the widest part was furthest from their bodies. Their single antreus each flashed silver. Andrielle always liked looking into their wings.

The depths of reflected colors mirrored the musical notes their quickened dispositions formed.

Wings meant fast escapes. Except that in Andrielle's case, she was incredibly lucky.

Gwen led the way to the Healer by taking the red low E flight path beginning right outside of her family's compartment through the cavern over to the yellow green natural G lane. Carl and Mitchell carried the litter. Madison and Pamela followed.

Justinda's compartment was lined with hive-like cubbyholes painted with beeswax. The honeyed fragrance combined with the aroma of sweet grass and soothed anyone who entered her home. Each cubbyhole was filled with healthy poultices and powders that Justinda had harvested from every latitude and longitude of the garden. On one side hung loose bundles of once blooming wildflowers so well preserved as they dried that they appeared to be just picked. Andrielle saw wormwood swatches, sage and bistort bundles. Those were the ones she could identify. There was a plethora of colorful dry bundles of which she had no idea what they were. A large vat of honey was stored next to another one containing softened beeswax. These were used to combine any dried herb into a poultice whose healing attributes cured the Candela whenever they came back hurt from their patrols. Candela were never beyond repair, as long as they could get back.

Andrielle slipped out of the litter and lowered herself onto the stool so that the Healer could inspect her wings. Justinda probed her left nicotinic flap, from which the left wing grew. It was intact, although sore. It was the right wing that was clearly damaged.

"I agree with your diagnosis as per usual, Gwen. Several of the right antrei need a poultice of chamomile and linden flowers, comfrey leaves, too. Beeswax will do for a binding. The torn tissues will repair and grow back within the interstitial laces. I'm confident that their color will restore as well. A couple of her antrei were almost fractured in half, the poultice will work on that, too. It's the nicotinic flap that worries me. It's nearly been pulled out of its socket. I'm prescribing traction, rest, tisanes of boneset and mullein. Andrielle, you can't fly for a while but your body will tell you when you're ready. When it doesn't hurt anymore." Justinda's matter of fact pronouncement helped them believe that Andrielle would soon be up and flying.

Andrielle tasted blueberry and chocolate sorbet when she realized that Pamela and Madison were looking at her with friendly sympathy. "Don't worry. We'll visit you all the time and spiral any color you'd like." They were sweetheart friends. Carl and Mitchell were angry. Mitchell especially.

"Who did this to you? Can you remember anything?" She knew instantly it was their anger that caused a bile taste in her mouth. Yuck, Candela gift of taste could be so annoying!

"I didn't see him. I think it was a him. First he pushed me down and I almost flipped over. I think he stepped on my wing. I thought he was going to start clubbing my head, but before I could get a really good look at his face, he flew away. I don't know that I'd recognize him if I see him again. Then, before I could fly away I tripped over bayberry roots and fell into the dry gravel bed. That's what really did me in. It happened so fast. But he didn't get any of my antrei." This last said with a stiff chin.

"Good for you, Andrielle."

"That'll show those Tureg."

"They'll be sorry one day!"

"Did you see what kind of wings he had?"

"What I could see, it looked like the two part kind, on the small side. His antrei had different colors all through, like mine, you know? Maybe they are rare in that fey?" Andrielle stopped and tears formed. "I never want to see him again!"

Andrielle was both terrified and looking forward to Gathering. She was going to give a report on her first official watch. She was not looking forward to giving testimony on her injuries.

Thank the seamless universe, though, she'd been spared.

~ Chapter 4 ~

Bret flew fast and furious toward the Tureg portal under the blue indigo. What in the garden had just happened there? He had done his duty. Footfall number eleven heard on the ground of the garden was the blaring signal he grimly waited for and secretly hoped would never happen on his watch. He'd only heard about it from older fey. His surge of anxiety to get on with it was laced with a tiny thread of fear. It wasn't that he was a coward by any means. He was, after all, the son of one of the Tureg's most worthy rescuers.

Bret did a quick flashback.

The sound he most remembered was the three bumblebees fighting in the next petal cavity bloom of the Rosa rugosa shrub. He couldn't tell if their stingers were actually piercing bodies, but by the horrendous sounds, there weren't going to be any bodies left. He remembered thinking, why does that species do that to themselves? He counted eleven petals on the rugosa and that alerted him to the eleven footfalls of the Candela walking on the ground under the bush, searching for something. Eleven—how dare it do that? The Candela wore its anklet on the left, too, what was that all about?

There were antrei just hanging off its wings and Bret felt a desperate urge to sweep in, grab and leave. There were ephemerals waiting! The color swirls above the Candela's wings were the sickening yellow and orange that typified that species of fey. Bret clutched his dogwood branch closer.

Swoop in, grab, and duck out. The Candela must have felt some inkling of tension in the air and turned around. Bret was suddenly blasted by a yellow wall of color. It filled his eyes and drove spikes into his brain. Sounds long and low, then high pitched, filled his ears. Around his neck might as well have been a hobnailed collar yanking him back. What in the forsaken universe was this? It was all he could do to keep from stumbling backwards and falling. He dropped his stick and flew away. Thank the seamless universe he managed to not trip over his own wings.

He flew back to the cavern on automatic pilot barely avoiding an eagle's nest at the last minute by dropping down under cover of scratchy pine trees.

As he flew he couldn't help but wonder about the other shocks. He had felt a smooth silky whirl of soft lamb's wool on his shoulders. The sight of a Candela only caused cold shivers at best. He tasted something, too, but he wasn't eating anything. It was the wild ginger tonic the Tureg enjoyed in moonlit ceremonies. Wild ginger was saved for reverent times, as opposed to, say, dandelion or juniper berry.

Why was he thinking about fey tonic? Looking at the Candela, he also grappled with numbers spiraling in concave and convex color colliding each and every way. The last thought he had was of a female face, a yellow explosion filling his senses until he felt lost.

He was pulled down into the light-filled Tureg portal. Everet, the portal keeper, looked worried at seeing Bret. They had grown up together in adjoining compartments, went to the same sequencing sessions. Even so, duty called for identification to be intoned and

Bret did so: 21 spirals as green as hail on limestone. Then he flew to his family compartment and hurriedly brushed aside the sweet grass tapestry covering the entranceway. Catching sight of his parents, Bret felt the caress on the side of his face that their closeness prompted and held onto them with all of his Tureg ephemeral hope. He was so desperately glad to see someone he could count on.

"What's wrong, son?" His mother's face started to reflect terrifying prime number sequences and they began to spiral. Bret knew he himself emitted the burnt orange color of the prime numbers 59 and 19. They blazed in his mind. It hurt.

"Mother! It was a Candela! It flew right into my perception by stopping on the eleventh footfall. We all know what that means. I dropped out from the fourth petal of the rugosa and was going to grab at it. But the Candela had its anklet on its left foot like we do. That stopped me for a minute. Then I tried to use my dogwood branch. The Candela fell into the loam and I could have harvested easily. Its wings were impressive. Many antrei were ready to fall off, so many ephemerals just waiting! They're going to waste away if we don't harvest very soon. I know that. But the flash of yellow was more than I could bear. It was the force of the sunflower spiral."

His mother stated the obvious, "It was the force of a well oiled trap."

"I could only fly away."

His father said, "Anything else, son?"

"Well, I don't know how to explain it. I think I heard some sounds but there was nobody else there. It sounded like all the wings in the garden waving at once, you know? And like our flute playing at ceremonies. And instead of feeling the usual scrape of broken teeth biting my ear that the Candela usually make me feel, I felt soft lamb's wool on my shoulder!"

"This is something!" mused his father. Selat looked at Sulpicett. "Perhaps ...?"

"Let's be careful about this," warned Sulpicett. "I don't think this will be welcome news in some corners of the Tureg." She glanced at her husband and caught his eye.

"Agreed."

"What are you talking about?"

"Never mind, Bret, nothing you need worry about. It's just that we Tureg now and then have these funny feelings. They don't last. I wouldn't put much stock in it and for the seamless universe's sake don't mention it to anyone else. They'll think you've seen too many long prime numbers." This last comment was accompanied with a knowing look to her son.

"There's something else, too." Bret still looked stunned.

"What is it, son?" his father looked intensely at his son.

"I tasted wild ginger!"

"Bret, how could you bring tonic on patrol!"

"No, that's not it. I wasn't eating or drinking anything!"

Selat's wings waved open and closed, projecting the deep blue of indigo and deep flame red of salvia. Thinking seriously did that.

"We're going to have to put this off until we can talk with Talandat. Don't mention it at Assembly."

Bret felt the tap on his shoulder and knew that Assembly was beginning, and he and his family flew down to the cavern.

His brother Colt and sister Margaret were waiting for them in the family number. 42 blazed turtlehead green and crimson king maple red, familiar and beloved. As long as he'd been Selat's and

Sulpicett's changeling he knew those colors, those numbers and the good backslaps and happy chin cuffs that his family and friends made him feel. Bret figured that today's Assembly would change those happy chin cuffs into slaps.

Talandat, Regent of the Tureg fey, was seated by his number, a large blue red 3, and began the Assembly by lifting up a cup of Tureg tonic made from elderberry and juniper. Each of the Tureg had a cup, even the most recently changed. Each sip drew the community together. Spectrum after spectrum of color spiraled together like a large and brilliant flame. Bret's family spiraled five different colors: green, blue, greenish yellow, bluish red, and gray. Gray since their family was gifted with rescuing ephemerals. Bret was still too much in shock. Today all colors revolved enough on their own.

"For our changeling health, for existing peacefully in this garden, for rescuing those that we can to our way of life, providing life and purpose from borrowed wings."

A low waving color began to spiral out in a gentle rhythmic sound like purring that stemmed from the movement of Tureg wings. All but Bret smiled and voiced their pleasure at the sweet caressing they felt on their cheeks, their shoulders and their arms.

Selat stood up and caught the eye of Talandat. "My sons Colt and Bret have reports to make."

Bret saw that all the Tureg were focused on him and he began the report. "The oil spill is cleaned up. My brother Colt can give you the details about the ocean floor. Zac and I alerted the beetles and they did the trick on the surface of the ocean."

Bret saw Colt stand up. "Talandat, Bret and I made a clean job of it. Of course, we did not do this alone. There was Zac, Jarret, Brant and Vincent who were with us. Jarret, Brant, and I were able to collapse the fissure on the ocean floor to stop the gush of oil. You should have seen it! It was worse than the last one!"

Talandat said, "I'm worried about the ocean floor. It's clear we need to step up our patrolling. I have to ask, did any raptors attack you?"

"There were some on the horizon, that's for sure. Osprey, I think, or maybe they were condors. We weren't bothered by them."

"I'm glad. The seamless universe only decreed that we fly, and fast, not that we have any other immunity from raptors. Remember, everyone, what happened to my son Stuart and always be vigilant, please."

All eyes turned to the Tureg seated at the side of Talandat between him and his wife Shalik and tried not to stare. Poor Stuart sat there with no wings. The story was that Stuart was patrolling a beach and was caught by two fighting egrets that had made a tug of war out of his wings. He was a reminder to all about the dangers fey faced every single day.

Bret spiraled his colors again. "I have another report. I was out harvesting antrei when I spotted a Candela as it stopped on footfall number eleven. There were several antrei ready to fall off. However, this Candela was really different. When it dropped to the loam a blaze of sun-drenched yellow from its face, like a sunflower, blind-sided me. Numbers began to swirl in a double helix. It was all I could do to limp backwards and fly back home."

"How could you not finish the harvesting?"

"Don't you know there are ephemerals wasting away?"

"They will die!"

A few of the Tureg council members began closing down their color spiral as the sorrowful knowledge began to sink in. Bret knew he'd be questioned at length by the council. There was no help for it. He had failed his Tureg mission.

From where he sat he could see the passage on the side of the cavern that led to the nursery. The two ephemerals he'd rescued earlier were purposefully transforming. Just one antreus meant restored health. Unfortunately, the number of waiting ephemerals was so large now, that he knew some of them were going to wait in vain.

~ Chapter 5 ~

Covered with poultices and medicated to the best of Justinda's ability, Andrielle joined her family for Gathering as they made their way over to the central area of the cavern. Magistrel, their Regent, took his place on his knobbed root chair situated at the highest point in the Gathering area. Nearby was the large knobbed root table where the Candela council sat. The Regent would hear all the reports before deciding on the issues of the day. Andrielle signaled her desire to speak by spiraling her colors and was recognized.

"Andrielle, you've made your first patrol. What is your report?" Magistrel spoke with a smile.

"Candela and council members, I took my first watch. I'll give my patrol report and then tell you what happened to me. I noticed that the count of pollinating bees was sparse. There were several species of bees that were not familiar to me, and they were much larger than our usual pollinators. I saw five different kinds that I recognized. And then I saw a sixth one. It was a huge bee with a proboscis that curled in and out. Its wings buzzed as fast as a hummingbird's. The sounds I perceived were chartreuse and salty. It must have been as big as me in this form.

"As to what happened to me, I think I know what the problem was. I put my anklet on the wrong foot and then I lost count of my steps as I walked on the ground. I thought I stopped on eight but it must have been the number eleven. I was under the Rosa rugosa. When I stopped, out of a petal cavity dropped a Tureg. He brandished a dogwood branch and that made me lose my balance. I fell into the gravelly earth. I scrambled around and tried to get away just in case they patrol by two, as I was taught to do. But then I stumbled over some large bayberry roots and tore up my wings in the worse kind of sharp gravel. By then, the Tureg was gone, I think he just flew away. I crawled to the ledge rock wall and back to the portal. My questions are, what is going on with the bees, and why did this Tureg just leave? He could have killed me easily. I didn't catch sight of him as I was mostly face down. I did see that he wore an anklet on his left ankle. That's when I realized my anklet was on the left. Maybe that was a cue to him, I don't know."

The cavern was filled with the Candela. They normally numbered 60, although this number varied over time. Tureg or raptors would catch some and that unfortunately depleted their population. Then, the Candela would increase with the addition of changelings. Changelings were their only hope, even though finding them was up to the seamless universe. Did the Tureg have trouble keeping their number stable? Did they die, too? The Candela knew little about the Tureg, except that time and time again the Tureg harvested antrei off of their wings. For the most part, the Candela recovered and the wing partitions grew back. Yet, sometimes the damage was so great, a Candela died. All of the changeling instructors warned the young Candela of the dangers that the Tureg posed.

Magistrel stood up. He was their oldest fey. It was rumored that he was one of the sparks out of the mouth of the first child who laughed. That was so long ago no one disputed it. He reached out to Andrielle with his arms, and his wings produced a serene intonation of honeyed middle C notes. The colors deep peach and true vermillion started a slow spiral up to the ceiling. Andrielle tasted sweet dandelion tonic as she looked up at him.

"For a long time now we have been in siege, which is why we carefully train you young fey to follow the ways we've set down. While on the ground, count your steps by two, stop only on even numbered steps, and never ever on footfall eleven. Intone no notes: fly with your color and music muted. Andrielle, you are instructed to sit through training again. I want you to review the whole process. We don't want you to have to rely on luck again."

Magistrel turned to his fey. "My dear Candela, our mission has always been clear: to observe human activity, to promote their and nature's seamless coexistence; to circumnavigate ceaselessly to thwart abuse to the garden when we find it; to help restore the balances in the seamless universe; to obstruct the harming of humans. Are there any other reports?"

Nathaniel stood up. He was a medium aged fey, with a generous red color spiraling up from his large waving wings. One could also hear the middle C humming in the background of his speech. Other fey turned to him as his color spiraled larger. Andrielle tasted honey made from wild thistle as she looked at him.

"I, too, noticed the increase of oddball bees and I wondered what was going on. So I flew over to where people were enjoying the forest preserve at Lake Kensington. I noticed that the emerald borers were plentiful there. Their activities are still as strong as ever eating away at the ash trees. My theory as to why so many different bees are now here is that their homes in the ash trees are being destroyed."

Many fey began intoning and Andrielle heard music soaring all over the cavern, with their attendant color spirals.

Magistrel said, "We'll have to watch the insect balance in the garden for a while to tell if the emerald borers have caused a definite imbalance or if it's merely a cyclical pattern with no real harm."

This was a good theory for the appearance of the bees. Now, what about the Tureg who could have killed Andrielle? Did they suddenly have a new disposition to the Candela? Probably not and like many in the Candela she wondered about peace with them.

What was this rift, this feud, this war, based on? It was a recurring question about which all Candela wondered. Andrielle had never been satisfied by the answers she'd heard. Her mother said it was over territory. Magistrel said they couldn't agree on music, color, taste and numbers. Numbers were usually touted as the major reason they'd been at war for so long. Tureg perceive numbers as color and a physical sensation. Yes, no wonder they hit so hard. While the Candela perceive music as color and tastes on the tongue. Music over numbers, numbers over music. Why should it make such a big deal difference?

After Gathering, the Candela retired to their home compartments. Andrielle lived with her mother Gwen, two older sisters, Julianna and Corrina, one older brother Daniel, and her father Cantrel. Each of them had been trained to observe the garden in its four elements: fire, water, air, and earth. It was Candela mission and what gave their existence purpose. The Candela had a rich heritage of seamless co-existence in this part of the firmament's garden especially now that people had built their homes here. Thus the fey purpose with regard to people had taken on a more gracious importance while the insect-plant balance that keenly reflected the health of the garden continued to be the main mission of the Candela.

Candela observations were reported to Magistrel at Gathering who in turn conducted executive council meetings to authorize investigations into repair of the fabric of the four elements. She knew that Magistrel was wise, but wondered about waiting to see what would happen where the bees were concerned. She also realized that she had so much to learn.

Candela were definitely aware of the other faction of fey, the Tureg, who lived in the garden, too. Over time, Candela began to believe that Tureg animosity meant they wanted Candela to relinquish their claim on this garden and move on to another one. Given their mission, most Candela were shocked that the Tureg would not work symbiotically with them for the good of the four elements. Not to mention the seamless universe. Candela and Tureg fought each other and Andrielle could not conceive of all of the reasons why, they were so deeply buried in the passing of time. She believed there was more to it. But what?

Her sisters Corrina and Julianna set the table with acorn tops, bowls of dogwood berries, elderberry tonic, and dandelion fluff marinated in honey with roquette and sorrel. Their brother Daniel was out on recon and would be back for dinner. Gwen and Cantrel took down their lutes and pipes to begin the music for dinner. No Candela meal was complete without music and dance. They began the circling steps around the room, bending low and arching high as they stepped and leapt and flew in time to the notes they composed. The three sisters began intoning their personal octaves. Soon the room was filled with the colors they radiated: Andrielle's sun-drenched yellow, Corrina's lobelia pink, Julianna's linden tree yellow green. Andrielle also tasted crunchy pine nuts from the Vanderwolf that grew over the ring of chanterelles in the hosta ridge that marked the Candela portal to their fey cavern. Cantrel's salmon red and Gwen's orange gold were well suited to their daughters' spirals. Daniel's brilliant bittersweet orange was what they needed to complete their family spectrum. Each compartment in the cavern was in its full blaze of color and lilt of sound when the families began their meals.

As Andrielle's family went about preparations for their dinner she thought a bit about being one of four children in their family. It reminded her that the Tureg who had caused her harm had made her sense the number 4. On top of that, she had tasted wild ginger flavored honey. Something pleasant from the Tureg – that seemed unlikely, yet there it was. To her recollection a Tureg had never inspired a true taste before. Anyway, nothing very pleasant. It was only your own fey who did that.

Also, the Tureg's color intoned a baritone low A.

The combination of taste and color and music was unusual in and of itself but the true mystery was why she sensed a number. This was near to shocking as far as she was concerned. She wanted to go to Magistrel's council meeting and seek advice.

The Candela executive council meeting met while the families were at dinner. All Candela but the five council members were in their compartments by the sound of soft music filtering down. Music that was the great symphony of the Candela.

She couldn't fly, so she had to walk. While her family was dancing and preparing for the meal and the arrival of Daniel, she took the stairs made by musical octaves and spiraling colors down to the floor of the cavern where she found the council in session at the knobbed-root table. She approached the council table and waited for them to notice her. These were the fey who decided all things for the Candela and all of them were dear to her.

Besides Magistrel, there was Quinn who sat next to Magistrel. She was an older Candela, maybe one of the few who remembered that there was a time before the feud with the Tureg. Even she hadn't explained the feud's beginnings to Andrielle's satisfaction. It was clear to Andrielle that Quinn knew something of how strange and complex the ties were between Tureg and Candela. She speculated that Quinn wished to find a way to re-foster friendship again. Of course she was strictly opposed in this by Bruce who sat across from Magistrel. Brian and Amanda flanked him. Brian, an older fey, was mostly worried about the dearth of Candela changelings. Amanda was the newest council member. She hoped for peace with the Tureg and consistently supported Brian in the cause to find a way to increase the number of Candela changelings.

Andrielle knew this because she had met with each of them during her training. Council members took keen interest that each young Candela held deeply felt convictions. Quinn caught Andrielle's eye as she waited to approach the council and they smiled at each other. At one time Andrielle had heard that she might have gone to Quinn and her husband Candoral, but apparently it was decided at the time that Cantrel and Gwen were due a changeling.

"Did you have an additional report to make, Andrielle?" Magistrel looked happy to see her.

"I did not mention something during Gathering, Magistrel. I wanted to tell the council in private. When the Tureg dropped out of the petal cavity of the rugosa I was almost face down. When I glanced up and saw him I tasted wild ginger flavored honey. And something else, I saw the number 4. Has a Candela ever done that before?"

Magistrel abruptly stood up. "Please, Andrielle, be very careful. Are you sure about this?"

"Oh, yes, I've tasted wild ginger flavored honey before, like in training sessions when we played with new changelings. But a number is something I've never sensed. The number 4 popped into my head out of nowhere. When did a Candela ever do that?"

Magistrel turned to Quinn, "Quinn? Haven't we waited for something like this? Andrielle, this may be the beginning of something quite extraordinary."

"Just wait a minute there, don't get so hopped up." From across the knobbed root table, Bruce looked very skeptical. "We've always had differences with the Tureg. Their propensity for numbers and hard physical touch is the streak of violence they can't control. They are very different than us. No matter if a Candela now and again senses a rogue number, we can never have peace. Don't get excited about some pie-in-the-sky reconciliation, it can never be. Andrielle is young. She can't be sure what she tasted. Ginger is an anti-inflammatory just like capsicum. Capsicum is, don't forget, the most highly toxic spice in the seamless universe. It'll eat you from the inside out just like acid."

"In milder forms capsicum is a curative so you might be out of line about that," Amanda said with a knowing smile.

"Look, Amanda, you're new around here. You're way too idealistic when it comes to these things. Don't waste my time on it." Bruce was shaking his head.

Quinn cleared her throat and spoke slowly, "Andrielle, are you absolutely sure about the taste and the number? Now take your time."

"Well, it happened fast. As soon as I turned over he flew off without even grabbing at my wings. Maybe he saw a dive-bombing hawk and wanted to get away. It was wild ginger flavored honey. Not too sweet, a little on the tart side—I love ginger that way. And a number? Why a number?"

"Did you see a 4 in your mind? Was it a color?" asked Brian. Experience had given him wisdom, and his cool head was appreciated.

"Um, come to think of it, it was green but an unusual type of green. Sort of like a eucalyptus leaf."

Quinn nodded. "A cool green rather than a warm green. Again, unusual for us. Andrielle, thank you for coming forward in executive council. We're going to have to discuss this among ourselves. If you don't mind, will you keep this information to yourself for a little while longer?"

"Oh, sure," Andrielle rubbed her shoulder. "I need to climb back up and rest. I'm starting to hurt again."

Hands came forward to help Andrielle up the color pathway to her family's compartment. Once she was gone Magistrel seriously intoned a baritone low A and spiraled orange red with spikey magenta threads.

"How can we keep this under wraps? What do you think, Amanda? You're our newest council member. You know how much we want to find a way to make peace with the Tureg." Magistrel turned to Amanda.

"I don't know enough about the problems between us and the Tureg. Sure, we have to find a way to make peace with them," she said, "but, I believe our real problem is changelings. We can't go on much longer as it is. Our numbers are dwindling and the few changelings we've managed to receive will not sustain us in the long run. What's going on?"

Magistrel and Quinn looked at each other. Some kind of decision must have been made between the two of them. Their yellow and red color spirals suddenly entwined while trumpet arias rang out.

Quinn began. "I knew that this day would come when the silent among us needed to speak." The council squinted at her and then looked at Magistrel.

Magistrel stood up and intoned middle A.

"Council members and colleagues, my dearest friends. It's been a long time since we've discussed the feud with the Tureg. Candela have come and gone, been replaced over and over. There are few who go back to the beginning of the firmament and, yes, I am one of those. What you don't know is that at the beginning of time the Tureg and Candela were colleagues and worked harmoniously together for millennia."

While Quinn sat pensively the rest of the council were quiet. Then something must have sunk in because they began discordant renditions of octaves not to mention weird color spirals that drenched the space. Magistrel didn't know about the rest of them, but the combination of red pepper and turmeric hit his mouth full strength. No one said anything, yet the looks on their faces said it all.

Magistrel went on, "Calm down everyone, there's more. In fact, our changelings are given to us by the Tureg."

Well, that did it. Amanda sat transfixed, while the rest of the council began shouting. "What are you talking about?" and "Who says so?"

Magistrel looked grim and said, "There's more. The Tureg rescue ephemerals from the humans and once they have them, they need our antrei. Our antrei possess the healing power to transform a changeling into fey. How many of you knew that?"

Magistrel knew better than to let this question hang in the air for long. "Our changeling symbiosis with the Tureg goes back to the beginning and has continued even after the rift with them occurred."

Bruce looked skeptical as per his usual manner. "By the firmament! If you've known this all along, why didn't you tell us? How dare you?"

"This could be the answer to our prayers," Brian looked astonished.

"Why can't we make our own changelings then? Why should we have to wait to see what's in the sweet grass field?" Amanda asked. "And by the way, what is an ephemeral?"

Magistrel held up his palms. "You need to understand it's only the Tureg who have the gift to rescue the ephemerals, the part of the human that can become changeling. Tureg bring that jewel of ephemeral hope to their cavern and use our antrei in the transformation. Candela or Tureg, it's all in the combination of antrei and ephemeral. Always a mystery why one over the other. I believe even they do not know how or why."

"Wait a minute! Maybe we should figure out how to rescue these ephemerals, and then try it ourselves," Amanda was smiling and nodding to Brian. "What do you say?"

"Why not? It can't hurt to find more out."

Bruce couldn't help shouting, "Are you crazy? It's been established since the time of the firmament, probably by decree of the original creative spirit itself! We have the wings, didn't you just hear what Magistrel said? They have the other gift, the one that counts—how ridiculous! You're going to find out nothing!"

"Magistrel, let us try!"

Quinn stood up. "This is why it's so important that we find a way to seriously communicate with the Tureg. We need them just as much as they need us. This is going to come as a great big surprise to the rest of the Candela. Judging from your reactions, Bruce, they are going to be shocked and angry. I hope they'll all be resigned, too. Resigned to finding a way to end the war." Turning to Magistrel, she asked, "Are you still in contact with Talandat?"

"What else are you keeping from us, Magistrel?" Bruce was rolling his eyes again.

"I've kept this from you to let time pass. To let tempers soothe."

"When are you going to let us in on why the feud started?"

Quinn answered for him. "Magistrel will be letting us in on all of that at the same time. And it better be soon. Right, Magistrel?"

"I'll find a way, just have a little more patience."

"So, what are we going to do?" Amanda summed it up best.

~ Chapter 6 ~

Bret glanced into the changeling nursery. Jondett was picking one up. It was one of the ephemerals he'd recently brought in, wrapped up in the silken blanket that the Candela antreus had become. Colors from the blanket flashed from green to yellow to orange to blue over and over again. When the flashing stopped, that meant the ephemeral was fully transformed and ready to open his or her eyes into a new world. Bret walked into the nursery and approached Jondett. He could see the look of joy as she held the ephemeral, as she smoothed the silken antreus around it.

"Bret." Jondett smiled as she saw him stride into the nursery toward her. "Come here and see. I think this one is going to be a Tureg. Whenever I stroke the cheek, color spirals up. I just know that it's sensing numbers or at least that's how it seems to me." Jondett held up the bundle to Bret and he took it into his arms. Wow, the numbers tumbled and soared, all kinds of colors were flaring.

"This is so amazing." Bret held the warm bundle up to look into its sleeping face and feel the colors flashing. He wearily thought of the ephemerals over on the right side of the nursery waiting for an antreus. He then looked at Jondett and saw the longing in her eyes. If all went well, they would be paired at the coming harvest and ready to begin their family lives till the end of time. The look in her eyes told him that it was both of their hopes to pair.

"Jondett, I have something very important I wish to ask you." Her endearing look, as she placed the ephemeral back into the milkweed pod, gave him courage. He gulped and said it. "I want to humbly express to you that I wish to pair with you, provide for us, and then when we are worthy to help all I am able with our own changelings. Above all, to initiate synchronicity with you so that time and again we grow closer to becoming one. Will you have me?"

"Yes, yes and yes!!" Jondett began to cry. Bret saw that they were tears of joy. "My mother knew this was going to happen. She just said the other day that she and your mother were talking about a pairing announcement party. Wait until I tell her that she can go ahead. She'll be beside herself, as will your mom." Colors were beaming around the nursery, all springing from Jondett's ecstatically flaring wings.

Bret knew he'd be throwing a big monkey wrench into the works, but it had to be done.

"Well, Jondett, there's something I have to take care of first. Well, I ... I have something to tell you and it's not good. I've only brought in four antrei this past week." Bret gestured to the little bundle in his arms. "I went before Assembly today." He gulped. "I told them what happened on my search in the garden."

Jondett's color stream abruptly stopped. "What do you mean? What happened? You're one of the best rescuers in all the garden."

"I just couldn't, well, didn't, gather any antrei from that last Candela I found."

"Are you kidding me? Don't you know what the punishment is for that?" Bret began to feel slaps on his arms, their strength increasing as Jondett talked to him.

"As if I didn't know."

"How dare you put this nursery in jeopardy—put me in jeopardy, too!" Slap.

"Why do you say that?"

"Excuse me, did you or did you not just propose that we pair and spend the rest of time together?" Slap, slap.

"Yes ..."

"It just so happens that you are probably going to Detention, Bret. If you wanted to pair with me, you didn't have to be so reckless. Are you sure you want to pair? Your actions tell a different story, you know." A bigger slap.

"Yes, Jondett, you're the only Tureg for me." The slapping stopped. Prime numbers began revolving.

"Oh sure. Time will tell. My mother is going to be furious. Now she'll have to wait, me too! For how long, Bret? For how long? And if that's not enough, there are so many ephemerals just waiting, still in their prairie smoke, thank the seamless universe. The two ephemerals you brought in—we were lucky that Zac had retrieved antrei from the sweet grass field. How could you?" Tears began to form in Jondett's eyes, falling as slowly as prime numbers revolved.

"Well, I have to answer for what happened at a justice hearing later on today."

"Oh my creative spirit, I just thought about something else." Bret had never seen Jondett so worked up. "They're going to say that maybe I should have put them on the ones waiting earlier, you know? I went out of order. I might be in trouble too!"

"Jondett, wait until I tell you. You're not going to believe this, but I was ambushed by the fierce color that struck me from the Candela I caught. I was walloped good. I'm still trying to figure it out. And here's something else, I tasted something. It doesn't make sense. We don't experience that!"

"When do you go to the justice hearing? Do you want me to go, too? I get off my shift here in four more time sequences."

"I'm pretty sure it'll all be over by then. When they're done with me, I'll come by and let you know what's going to happen." Bret walked away from the nursery with a sense of foreboding. The justice council was strict but fair. One never got anything that wasn't due.

At the council meeting, everyone was resigned and even a bit sorrowful. Much to their credit, no one gloated. Not that it mattered since the punishment had been established for eons. The trip to Detention was Bret's first, and the trip there wasn't that bad. Bret surveyed the surroundings in the deep water. This trench was the deepest in the Atlantic Ocean near the island land mass the people lately called Puerto Rico. He had patrolled the trench before, and there wasn't much down here, just some big toothed translucent fish. They looked really horrible, but they scurried right away.

Maybe it wouldn't be so bad. He could breathe under water. After all he was fey. He'd stay away from the aggressive Tureg incarcerated here, and try to make connections with the odd creatures that guarded the trench. There were the sea dragons, the ghostpipefish and something that looked like a string of lights slowly zigzagging along the edges. Strange creatures lived down here in the depths.

For all the garden, besides the snake-like string of lights, the others looked like glistening seaweed with a face. He could see through their bodies as if they were a leafless bush, like an underwater tumbleweed. Nothing underwater seemed to stay still even for a minute. The rocks appeared to move back and forth in the water. Doubtless due to the bits and pieces of fluctuating greenery attached to them.

Nobody in Detention could spiral colors and numbers. It was part of the punishment. It felt awful. It was supposed to help them listen to the lectures without distraction. Maybe that was true. However, it was so unnatural it caused him to have weird depressing dreams. He vowed to never miss out on harvesting antrei again, no matter what. He could barely stand the ache he felt deep in his solar plexus.

His bunkmate was Zac. He had done exactly what Bret had done, neglected to harvest antrei. Putting the ephemeral nursery in jeopardy was a major crime. Perhaps the two of them might be back in the garden soon because they were among the very best at harvesting antrei. At least that's what they hoped, just like everyone in prison who wanted early release. If not, they were in for a long wait for a pairing and then for a changeling of their own. Bret hoped that Jondett would wait for him. At least that's what she tearfully vowed at their last meeting. He wondered who it was that Zac had waiting for him.

Thinking about Jondett make him realize that yes, he was worthy to pair and hope for a changeling. Only the worthy among the Tureg were eligible. Bret smiled as he remembered what he and Zac did one time to prove themselves, something he knew they never should have risked doing: capturing an egg from a raptor's nest. It was something all Tureg kids worth their juniper wanted to do, even though the council repeatedly warned against it. Tureg could be killed right inside the raptor nest, for the garden's sake!

If you really could steal an egg, wow, was that a bragging right! Two years ago he and Zac defied the council and went for it. They flew up into the high branches of a Norwegian pine, where an eagle's huge aerie precariously hung. They took one egg out of the many and cared for it until the hatchling cracked its way out of its shell. What a job, especially since it had to be kept secret. The idea was to be there at the moment of birth and look at the hatchling eye to eye so that a bond was formed. No raptor born like this could ever take a fey, it was said.

The eaglet had pecked its way out of the hard shell, and once it opened its eyes, it saw Bret and Zac. Then the two Tureg transported the nearly bald hatchling back to its nest where the eagle parents would take it back in, they figured. They had to wait until both parents were momentarily away. Then they put the newly hatched eaglet under one of the unhatched eggs and hoped for the best.

When the news got around the cavern, Bret and Zac incurred wrath from their Regent and the council like never before. Their punishment was that they had to clean out and scour the gathering space without the help of Tureg power. That was a miserable punishment. On top of that, the eaglet was never seen by any Tureg again, so what was the point of it all? He had learned his lesson. Now he was here, enduring his first punishment in Detention, learning another lesson he should have taken to heart long ago.

The surroundings were lit with phosphorescent fish. The swing of colorations was actually beautiful, and now and again this made him forget that he was not allowed to spiral color. Tomorrow would start the lectures. He would go at it with determination, with such a pure heart that his sentence might be shortened.

Outside, the ocean creatures peered in at the fey, a zoo in reverse. Wait, thought Bret, we're invading their water. We are *their* zoo.

Bret went down to the dining room. Cancret was waiting there. "Ha, look who's here—the very Bret who thought he was better than me. No violence he used to say, don't rip the wings off the Candela, they don't deserve that. And yet, here he is, the big shot. You didn't get the goods either. You better believe Candela don't get away from me."

"You weren't there, so back off. Besides, you one-winged bully, you're still wrong, you're not supposed to kill them."

Bret saw several inmates surround Cancret. There was Wyatt who had torn half the wings from a Candela leaving it helpless. Next to Wyatt hunkered Trent, a strapping young Tureg who had followed Wyatt into the garden hoping to learn how to harvest antrei. In the process he was caught in the middle of beating a Candela nearly to its death. He didn't seem to want to criticize Bret and held back. Maybe there was hope for Trent.

Then there was Gerhardt, a very muscled Tureg who clearly would scare the wits out of any Candela. He was here because of what his large hands could destroy. One time Gerhardt left a Candela totally shriven of one whole wing. Bret had heard that it wasn't the first time, either. It was about time Gerhardt was caught.

The first and foremost reason for being sentenced was not harvesting antrei when available. Harming a Candela was the second, and to Bret, the most grievous reason.

Now these bullies were after Bret, who had given them reason to be jealous back home.

"Steady, guys," Bret looked worriedly from one to the other Tureg surrounding him. "We're on the same side, remember?" Bret saw them raise hunks of calcified coral and he could almost feel the punches those clubs would inflict.

The big bruisers advanced toward Bret when suddenly they stopped and hung paralyzed, their calcified coral clubs held high. One by one they toppled and fell down. Between the wings of each Tureg was a yellow leafy sea dragon. These were the wavy yellow creatures he'd noticed at the edge of the ocean floor dining area. Clearly Bret had underestimated what seaweed with a face could do. Or how fast they could move.

Bret moved away from the dining area with a cautious backward glance at the paralyzed Tureg fallen in heaps on the ocean floor. The sea dragon on Wyatt disconnected and made its way to Bret, who covered his face. Wonder what's going to happen to me, he thought, if they can do that to our strongest meanest Tureg.

"We don't like to do that," the sea dragon said. "My name is Cam, and I'm the head of security here. Now and then we have to prevent fights. You Tureg sure are mean when you want to be. Why is that?"

"Don't ask me, I'm not like them."

"That's what they all say."

"Wait a minute. Sure I'm supposed to be here, but I didn't cause any Candela to die or lie helpless."

"Oh, is that right? That's not what I heard."

"Well, I did push one Candela down and all, but I'm pretty sure it was able to get away. I don't know for sure ... I was so stunned I could only fly away. Those guys over there," pointing to the big Tureg on the floor, "they love beating up a Candela. They like nothing better than to rip off the wings, and leave it. They don't care that a Candela dies or can't move. My crime, and yeah, I know it's wrong, is that I didn't get any antrei when I could have. There were lots that looked like they were going to fall right off. It would have been easy." Bret stopped for a minute and his forlorn look deepened. Then he continued, "Just shake the Candela a bit and they'd have fallen off onto the ground. Oh, my garden, ... why didn't I ... there are so many ephemerals just wai..."

Bret felt Cam land on his shoulders momentarily. Relief flooded his system as the sea dragon floated away.

So that's their gift.

Sleep came easily after that for Bret. The last thing he saw before falling blissfully asleep was his cellmate Zac who lay on his bunk staring out into the deep indigo of the ocean depth, wings tucked underneath him. Ghostpipefish and sea dragons hovered luminescent at the edge of their vision, no doubt looking for a swirl of prohibited color or a flash of numbers.

The next day Tureg eyed each other over their breakfasts, shrugging and nodding. They were all tranquilized, they sure looked it. Now that Bret knew first hand what sea dragons could do, he felt safer. Cancret, their ringleader, was sipping something out of a bottle. All wings waved smoothly, colorlessly, numberless.

Right after breakfast the lectures began. Lectures about the balances in the earth-air-water-fire elements of the seamless universe. Lectures about their mission as Tureg. Blah, blah, blah. It occurred to Bret that perhaps there should be a prison for the Candela. After all, wasn't it their fault that Tureg landed in Detention in the first place? If Candela did not withhold their antrei, the Tureg wouldn't need to go on patrol and take them. The balance of continuing fey in the universe was at stake here. Bret had not heard of a Candela Detention. Did one even exist? Or were the Candela blithely unaware of the part Tureg played in ephemeral rescue or change-ling existence. Did they even know that the Tureg gave them their own changelings?

Cam pointed to a map, "Listen up. This garden we call Earth has layers called continental plates that shift around causing earth-quakes and plenty of other trouble. It all begins with those Dantorak. How many here have heard of the Dantorak?"

Bret blinked in confusion. He hadn't. Had anyone else? What was Cam talking about? Besides all the Tureg who'd tried to bash him in, and Zac, there were two others from the cavern. No one raised a hand.

"Well, little fey, let me clue you in." Cam looked scathingly at the small group of Tureg seated in front of him on the ocean floor. "You think you don't like each other? You think you and the Candela don't like each other? You think you've got problems? Let me tell you – those are nothing compared to the Dantorak. For one thing they're fey. But that's where the similarities end. They don't like you guys, they don't like humans, and they don't want you or them to exist on the face of this garden. See, they believe it's because of you that this garden is in trouble. You clean up the problems people cause, and they don't like that. They're capable of instigating another ice age, the warming of the firmament, more cataclysmic volcanic action, stuff like that. You heard about the wipe out of all the dinosaurs? That was them! You heard about the last ice age ten thousand years ago? That was them! Every earthquake, every hurricane, every tornado, that ... was ... them!"

"You're crazy!" Gerhardt stood up from the boulder he was perching on. "There's nobody but Tureg and Candela in this garden!"

"Poor ignorant fey – there's more unknown than known about the garden. The Dantorak live deep in the cavernous center of the earth and revere this garden as much as you do. However, they believe that there is not a shred of evidence that people will ever contribute to the seamless universe, so they cause shifts in the garden's deep crevasses and make the people take notice. I worry that one day causing only a few to die won't be enough for them. The Dantorak will be out for blood, you can count on that. Only a few humans are aware that they are at the mercy of the havoc the garden can wreak. But humans are here to stay, and Tureg and Candela are here to stay. You all have to get along!"

"I don't believe you!" yelled Cancret. "You're just making up a story."

"I wish I was. They constantly try to disrupt your works. They hope that by you coming here to Detention, about which they know, that you'll see the error of your ways, join up with them and stop humans in their tracks, too."

"So, what do they look like, what are they like, these Dantorak?" said Bret as he shot a worried look at Cam.

Cam pulled down a screen. "Here's a drawing compiled from the few eyewitnesses. As you can see they look something like Tureg. Candela, too, for that matter, but no wings. They fly, they can do everything fey can do, since they are fey, but no wings. On the other hand, they are not male or female. They are gifted with neutrality."

"Yeah, but they're not neutral about the people," remarked Bret.

Zac said, "Do they have families, do they raise changelings?"

"When their numbers are low, they look to the humans. Those who are lost in some way, doing no good in the garden, self-destructive. Of course according to them, that more or less means most of humanity. But the ones that are most at risk of being taken are the ones that dip into the earth. Humans that dig coal, dive deep into the ocean, especially if they are depleting any resource. Believe it or not, they just take the human by collapsing one down into a Dantorak. The Dantorak are full adults from the beginning of their fey existence."

"Let me get this straight," Gerhardt cracked his prodigious knuckles. "They spring forth fully formed into fey. How do they know what they're doing?"

Zac said, "Is there a training period, like we have?"

"Just let me at one, I'll show them what for." Cancret always got down to basics.

"Cam, why are you telling us this?" said Bret.

"You have to know what you're up against. You Tureg and Candela have to find a way to work together. The Dantorak love nothing else than to disrupt whatever you do to heal anything."

"Sounds like our real enemy," Zac looked shaken.

Magistrel met Talandat at the agreed upon place in the middle of the field of sweet grass. It was a revered area of the garden and few Tureg and Candela were allowed there until the time of harvest. Soon gatherers from each fey would reap huge bales of the fragrant herb. Separately, and far away from each other, they'd gather and dry armfuls on top of ferns and woodruff. Once dry, the fey would craft baskets, mats and wall hangings for their caverns. The dried sweet grass provided much needed vessels for both Tureg and Candela, and bonfires for nighttime ceremonies. After harvest, the pairing off ceremonies were conducted here, too, separately. The rampant suspicion, the feud, the mistrust – it was such a waste.

Both Magistrel and Talandat smiled with satisfaction that the sweet grass was growing well. There was a time when Tureg and Candela combined in effort, happy and carefree, each helping the other in a bountiful harvest.

"How I wish our fey could solve our differences before harvest," Magistrel began with the usual lament.

Each time they met, one or the other began their conversation like that. They understood each other since both Magistrel and Talandat had begun their fey life during the first laughter, when fey first began. Whirling away as sparks in the dark immensity of the universe, they coalesced into form and matter. Magistrel and Talandat found themselves on the firmament together. And together, they came to this garden when gardens first sprang from the firmament, beginning their fey existence at the same time, in the same place.

Neither of them had been able to help their respective fey come to terms with each other. Also, as he'd done each time he and Talandat had met, Magistrel placed a wrapped package at the side of the boulder. His own discarded antrei glowed through the wrapper.

"And so, dear friend, my Andrielle was hurt on patrol. Her wings are special, even in the Candela. It's been a long time in the garden that such fine blazes of color such as hers appeared."

"I know all about it. It was Bret. He was struck by the force of the sunflower spiral and fled before he could take some of her antrei. They are sorely needed in the nursery but he could do nothing else but fly away."

"Well, she's convinced herself that it's all his fault. Although she did concede that she fell into the gravel and that was really the cause of her injuries."

Talandat began pacing around the boulder. "At the moment he's in Detention." Talandat continued pacing for a few moments, lost in thought. Then he stopped and looked at Magistrel. "Something else happened to Bret out in the garden. He sensed a taste – what do you make of that?"

"Andrielle told the council about sensing a number, too." Magistrel had his chin in his hand while he sat. "I'm wondering if this is the beginning of something."

"We've been disappointed before."

"What if this is different?"

"You always say that, and we get our hopes up, and then we're disappointed."

"I know."

"Time will tell."

Both Talandat and Magistrel looked at each other with some bemusement, and shrugged.

~ Chapter 7 ~

It was only by chance that Magistrel let slip during Gathering that the Candela had to do something drastic, given the sparse number of Candela changelings recently. Magistrel clamped a hand over his mouth. Maybe it was the seamless universe that made him say it. He looked around to see if anyone noticed, and, yes, wide opened eyes focused on him. Colors stopped flashing and hung in the air in anticipation. Magistrel felt like all the rainbows in the garden were arcing toward him.

Bruce began, "Now that you mention it, Magistrel, hasn't everyone worried that our number dwindles, while replacements are fewer and fewer? I think those Tureg are to blame. No matter where changelings really come from, I think Tureg snatch them up from the sweet grass field before we can claim them. We need to step up our patrols, for the garden's sake." Magistrel realized that Bruce was prompting him to come clean. That knowing look, those raised eyebrows said it all. It was time. Maybe he's right, Magistrel sighed.

Pamela spoke up, too. "Magistrel, I want to pair with Carl at this coming harvest. We want nothing more than a chance to raise a changeling and will pledge to the seamless universe that we will raise ours to grow into the beautiful mission that Candela were gifted with. If we don't get one, the Tureg are to blame!" Shouts began and then a discordant blast worthy of a crashing avalanche pummeled the cavern.

"Calm down, my dear Candela." Magistrel looked a bit resigned. "Perhaps it's time for all of you to know something. I can't let this go on any longer. Sit back, and hear what I have to say to you." Quinn sat next to him, grim and pensive. Bruce rolled his eyes, Brian and Amanda looked full of hope.

Andrielle and her parents were among the ones who looked at each other and wondered what Magistrel was going to say. Might it be about the new ability that Andrielle seemed to possess? Andrielle was terrified that all eyes were suddenly going to switch from Magistrel to her. It wasn't fair, she thought. She'd only had her first patrol in the garden. Was it really her fault that it went so wrong?

"A long time ago, long before most of you became Candela, there were always fey, our own and the Tureg. Have you ever wondered about the way Candela increase in numbers? Or, why? Our change-lings are found in the sweet grass. Our finding Candela bring them to our nurseries where they are eventually given to responsible Candela pairs. Changelings are our most precious resource, and doesn't it appear that the seamless universe itself gives them to us? As if somehow we are deemed so worthy, changelings just fall into our hands. Most of you are not aware that it is the curious blend of chance and circumstance that we have possession of any Candela changelings at all.

"The Tureg ... now don't start clanging and blaring, please. They are in fact at the heart of the matter. You know from your training classes to avoid them at all costs. You know to count your footfalls, and wear an anklet on your right foot. And you know that now and again, Tureg attack us, for no reason other than it's an ongoing war of sorts. They've caused many of you to be fearful, resentful, antagonistic to those who cause you harm. Sometimes even death has occurred at the hands of a Tureg."

Mitchell's colors flared far above the gathering, signaling to Magistrel that he would like to speak. Magistrel nodded.

"Magistrel, a prime example of this is poor Andrielle here. Her wings are torn and it's all because of a Tureg!" This only let loose angry shouts of defiance toward the Tureg. There were lots of screechy high notes, and grumbly scratchy notes, hardly music at all.

"So true, so true, and it's my fault, my dear Candela, for letting this go on for so long. To my only defense, I thought that things were going along pretty well, but now it's all so out of control. Candela have died because of raptors and at the hands of Tureg. We can't do anything about the raptors; the seamless universe gave us that to deal with the best we can. But there is something we can do about the Tureg. We can heal the problems between our two fey. We depend on them more than you think. This war has gone on too long."

All Candela at Gathering sat electrified. Magistrel was going to reveal something of major importance. Most of them had never heard him do that.

"I'm at fault for keeping from you an enormous universal truth. There were reasons for that. Reasons that by now have become mere flaccid reminders of jealousy, of hard-heartedness, of such self-centeredness that it will surprise you. What I'm about to reveal to you, I hope you take to heart in order to commit yourself to do what must be done."

Quinn put her hand on Magistrel's shoulder and gazed at him. Her look was full of sad courage, of pride in him. The rest of Magistrel's council sat grim and stoic.

"My dear Candela, our changelings are due to the fine work of craftsmen which entitles us to changelings."

A flare up of color caused all to look at one Candela at the middle of Gathering. "Are you saying that there are Candela who do this work for us?"

"In actual fact, the reason we have any Candela changelings at all is due to the nurturing hard work of the Tureg fey."

Shouts ranging from "You can't be serious!" and "Are you crazy!" to "What in the garden is he talking about?" and "Magistrel, you've lost your mind, somebody get the healer!" were heard all over the Gathering space.

Colors were flaring and spiraling all over the place, and out of control. Discordant music from the minor to the major keys blared and blatted. Light spectrums broke apart, crashing into each other as the colors flared as brightly as magnesium strength and as muted as muddy river bottoms. Candela everywhere were tasting bile. It was horrible to hear from the lips of their beloved Regent that the very essence of Candela life was dependent on their sworn enemy.

Quinn and Brian stood up and tried to be heard over the din. Quinn offered, "Friends, listen, please, Magistrel has more to tell you." Brian appeared agitated as he said, "It'll be fine, don't worry, you'll see, there's an explanation. Listen and quiet down."

Finally, Magistrel gained the attention of Gathering as Candela color and music wove into sync and calmed down. Magnesium-strength light shows softened and the color of dark chunks of mud became café au lait smooth. Dissidence mellowed from canon shot to whispers through the leaves. Vomit and bile became tansy and woodruff tea, bitter but tolerable.

"What would I give to not have to tell you this? The Tureg, you will see, are not the enemy you think they are, but indeed things have gone on for millennia and are so far in the past that only with true Candela perseverance and compassion can we get past what we need to get past. Here is the story."

Magistrel proceeded to enthrall the Candela as only he could do. "After the first fey were formed on the firmament, our two groups came to reside in this garden. We were known as Candela and Tureg. Our differences were noted and that became the reason two separate groups were formed. We spiral music as part and parcel of our lives. We taste things when we're happy – wonderful things when we're happy. A terrible taste in our mouths results when things are not so happy, right?"

Magistrel looked around and saw with satisfaction that Candela were taking sips from their tonic cups to rinse out the bile taste. He needed to do that, too.

Magistrel continued. "The Tureg don't spiral music like we do. They spiral numbers and equations, the sum and substance of the seamless universe. Instead of the gift of sensory taste their thoughts and emotions give them physical sensations. Sometimes bruises result from punches they don't see. They feel punches when they're confronted by a heartrending situation, like death from a raptor. We're not the only ones harassed by raptors. They feel hugs when they're happy. Anyway, because of our differences we developed into separate communities and yet connected. We each sought to protect the seamless unity in the garden. We both observe and have jurisdiction over different parts of the land mass and water mass.

That way the entire garden is covered. Separate missions exist to this day. For instance one thing we observe is the insect/bird/plant balances. Haven't you ever wondered what happens to the water/firmament balances? All four elements of the seamless universe are covered by both of our two fey. What also exists to this day is the way in which our changelings are formed."

Pamela flared her colors, sounded a trumpet aria, and Magistrel nodded for her to speak. "Magistrel, are you saying that it's up to the Tureg whether or not I shall be a mother?"

"Not really, Pamela." Magistrel smiled at her with pride. "Candela depend on the responsible among us for this beautiful self sacrificing choice to parent a changeling." He turned to the entire group. "Look at your wings, all of you. They are of many colors or they are of one color. There are many antrei or there is only one antreus in your wings. You know what happens to our wings. Each individual antreus sloughs off when they mature and when a new one has grown to take its place. It's sort of like people losing their baby teeth and growing adult teeth but we grow antreus after antreus. There's no discomfort to any of us when we lose an antreus, it just falls off.

"Those antrei are integral to the process of new changelings. My dear Candela, our wings change an ephemeral into a changeling. Oh, it's more complicated than that, but essentially without our antrei, changelings do not come into being. Our wings are more precious than any new color we can fashion from the aurora borealis and more precious than a new species found at the vast depths or endless edges of our garden."

Amanda stood up. "It's true, Candela. Without us and our wings, no new changelings would ever be formed from the ephemerals."

Intense mutterings could be heard all over the gathering space:

"Ephemeral?"

"What's that?"

"What is he talking about?"

Magistrel explained, "When I said that our changelings are our most precious resource I sidestepped the most precious of all ... the ephemeral. Ephemerals are a part of those just born human babies who soon die, or human babies who die before they are born. They are so loved by their human mothers and fathers that their life intensity spirals color after color – like we do! So much color that a patrolling Tureg is alerted. That Tureg rescues the glowing ephemeral and takes it to their Tureg nursery where it is cared for until it transforms into a changeling."

Notes started to flare again and shouts could be heard. "So that's why we have so few Candela – the Tureg are stealing all of them!"

Magistrel tried again to contain the shouting, and when the Candela had settled down, Bruce continued. "That's not it at all, for the seamless universe's sake. Now settle down. They can't keep all the changelings, both Candela and their own. How could they care for ours? For that matter, what would we do with a Tureg changeling? Can you imagine?" Candela started to laugh at the thought.

Quinn advised, "Perhaps an explanation on how one can tell a Tureg changeling from a Candela?"

"Yes, I will. My dear Candela, it's a lot more complicated than we can imagine. Simply put, with the help of our antrei the ephemeral becomes a changeling, Tureg or Candela depending on what colors the fully formed changeling swirls. Tureg changelings swirl the cool colors and Candela the warm colors. Soon after, all fey radiate a balance of warm and cool colors as you can see around you. Yet we Candela use the warm spectrum more. Plus, we sense music, they don't. We sense taste, and they do not." All colors of the spectrum were swirling and waving in the gathering place like so many rainbows glistening. All Candela were hovering, speechless, colors morphing up and down the color spectrum. Octaves of music soared all through the cavern and provided a welcome background tapestry of sound.

Andrielle signaled to speak and Magistrel allowed her.

With an incredulous look Andrielle asked, "Does this mean that the Tureg was only after the parts of my wings that were falling off?"

"More than likely. Or, the Tureg was out looking for discarded antrei. When ones fall off here inside our cavern they are taken outside to the sweet grass field as if to get rid of them. In reality Tureg gather them and take them to their nursery."

"Why don't we just give them to the Tureg, then?" quivering cries went up all over the gathering place.

"At one point in our history that was the way it was done."

"What happened?"

Quinn stood up and said, "Tureg and Candela lived in peace and harmony for a long time. We took care of all four elements in the garden – together. We helped heal and soothe the effects of terrible disasters in the garden, such as wildfires, earthquakes. It was a wonderful co-existence. The two fey cannot pair but we were dependent on one another in one of the finest alliances in the seamless universe. True harmony."

Magistrel resumed speaking. "Unfortunately, we came to a disagreement. I so wish we could go back in time and correct what we did."

"How could we have ever dreamt that it would go so far?" Quinn said.

"It was their fault, too," sighed Bruce.

"No," shot back Magistrel with full voice and flaring color. "It was all our fault!" Turning to the gathering, Magistrel continued. He looked as angry as the Candela had ever seen him. All those who'd flown up, flew back down to huddle with their family groups. They sat as still as stone to hear him talk.

"It came to pass that we lost a number of Candela and few of our changelings were forming. No one can predict what an ephemeral will become, but at that time our numbers were low. I think we were down to about 40, very low. The Tureg on the other hand were abounding in changelings. Their numbers were well over 100. Some began to think that the Tureg were keeping our changelings from us, or worse yet, somehow not allowing ephemerals to develop into Candela. And then when it came time for the competition ..."

Quinn bent toward Magistrel and whispered in his ear. "Yes, I will," Magistrel was heard to remark.

"My dear Candela, you will like this, I'm sure. In those far happier times, Tureg and Candela engaged in a friendly competition after harvest. Such a fruitful time. New colors were born, stars were named, new ideas sprang forth, dreams led to wishing led to revealing new species of flowers, or insects, and even sea life. We Candela used our music to find a new star song, or the song of waterfall. All for the betterment of the seamless universe.

"Well, because of our low numbers we were not doing well. Then, during the 'Locate a new star in the universe' competition, an actual new star was discovered. Very impressive, and you must understand that a discovery like that is not unheard of but it is rare.

The winning fey can name the star. It would have been in good taste for the Tureg to have named the star after the Candela fashion. But the Tureg in question was a bit young, and decided to name the star after his mother. Really, was that so terrible?"

There were shouts from Gathering: "That's all?" "How ridiculous!" and "I can't believe it!"

"Well, my dear Candela, there is more. In those days, one of the competitions was to find a plant in the garden that both Candela and Tureg could benefit from. And so it came to pass that the Candela brought back a new species of calla lily. Like the usual calla lily these were made up of one very sturdy petal. The difference in this one was that it dried to perfection. Both Tureg and Candela could use them in construction. They're very common now. You can see that they are used all through our cavern for canopies and vats, that sort of thing. The Candela brought back armloads and verified where the new calla lily grew."

"Did the Tureg find anything?" a querulous cry from the back.

"Well, they did find something, too. They found a new species of saffron growing on the lower peaks of the Himalayan Mountains. The honey made from a combination of the stamens of the saffron and Edelweiss that grows in the Austrian Alps is extraordinary. Mixed then with the fruit of ginseng it makes delightful tonic. Its benefits include being an antidote against infection. Well, the Tureg produced the tonic for all to partake, and a fight broke out when the Tureg taskforce would not divulge where the plants grew. Not really much of a problem in the long run since our Candela taskforces have come across the contested plant ourselves, and we make our own honeyed tonic. And yet, given the times, our fey were insulted, left the field and never looked back. Their Regent's name is Talandat.

He and I were not Regents at that time and could not persuade our fey to stop fighting. We swore to each other that if and when we became Regents we would work toward reconciling.

"The damage was and continues to be horrendous. Where once the antrei of our wings were gladly and freely given, the Tureg now have to search for them. Sometimes they have to grab them off our wings. It's only so that they can go back to their nurseries and wrap an ephemeral."

"Candela have died—we've been hurt!"

"Yes, things have gone beyond what the seamless universe can endure. Some Tureg have become horribly aggressive. We hide and withdraw like cowards who don't confront but merely talk behind the enemy's back. It's the worst kind of miscommunication. Tureg are at their wits' ends to have our antrei. No doubt, you will like this, too: Tureg go to prison, it's called Detention, for harming a Candela. Andrielle's attacker is in Detention as we speak paying for his crime. There are two crimes: number one, hurting or killing a Candela; and number two, not retrieving antrei when they're available."

Fey were taking this in, some shaking their heads, some weeping.

Andrielle noticed that Magistrel was not alluding to the fact that she sensed a number. Wasn't he going to tell Gathering about that? She wove and flared a brilliant orange but Magistrel ignored her and shot her a knowing glance, and an upraised finger. Fine, not here. All right, but she needed some answers.

After Gathering, Magistrel followed the stairs to his compartment in the cavern, taking the high C path to his light blue and lemon yellow space. Ever since the beginning of the firmament these had been his colors, and he loved them. All his changelings used them, too. His beautiful wife, Colima, sat combing her long silver hair by the glowing mica of the fireplace. Her wings drooped to the floor in rivulets of crystalline color. Clearly she was relaxed and happy.

"Ah, there you are, you big boolah," Colima and Magistrel had used silly nicknames for each other ever since their pairing.

"Now, boochey," Magistrel said as he wagged his finger at her. "What am I going to do with you?" His smile crinkled the sides of his face. He could depend on her to lighten up any dark mood.

"Tell me what happened at Gathering. I should have been there." Colima looked at Magistrel with her upturned face, holding a lemon verbena wooden comb in her long graceful fingers.

"Well, you're not going to believe it, but I finally let the Candela know about the Tureg, our competitions, and all about ephemerals turning into changelings."

Colima dropped her comb, which clattered against the quartz crystals lining their cavern. "It's about time! I could never understand what you were waiting for."

"For time to pass. For the jealous loud mouths among us to wise up. For the seamless universe to dump a load of basalt rock on me." Magistrel sat down at their table looking for all the garden like he'd lost his last friend. "I think the news sat well, after a fashion..."

"Oh, sure it did! I can only imagine."

"...I think it'll be all right in the end. It had to happen. It's gone on far too long, we all know that."

Magistrel could tell that Colima was going to tell him something he didn't want to hear. She straightened up, set a line in her lips, and gave him a stern look.

"Now we can finally have an understanding between us and the Tureg. We can finish the competition that set us both asunder."

"Now, boochey," began Magistrel.

"Don't you boochey me! You know what you have to do."

Magistrel knew what he had to do, and it was high time. He set off at once to the meeting place in the sweet grass where he and Talandat had always met.

~ Chapter 8 ~

Magistrel found Talandat sitting on the basalt rock boulder as if he had not left since the last time they met. It was good to see him again even though it wasn't the usual time for their conversation. Talandat raised an arm in greeting. His blue green robes slightly fluttered in time to the miniscule quivering of his large lobed wings.

"Ah, old friend, what brings you here so early? I wasn't expecting you. Several of my Tureg are here to bring changelings to the fields for your finding Candela. Better be careful they don't see you."

"You will not believe what just happened in our Gathering. I finally told the Candela – it was an accident, believe me, but I really had no choice and it looked like the seamless universe somehow manip..."

"Slow down – you're going way too fast. What happened?"

"The Candela now know what went wrong between our two fey."

Magistrel could tell that he had his old friend's attention. Talandat's colorful numbers shot up to the tops of the sweet grass and flashed from blue to red to orange. Hot colors far afield of his usual cool ones.

"You and I and a few others know the real story. Now the entire Candela know. They are stunned to say the least, and still angry that the whole feud has led to maiming and deaths of Candela. More importantly, they also know that the Tureg give us our changelings. That piqued everyone's interest to say the least."

"Do they know about the Dantorak, too?"

"No, I thought two shocks were enough. A third one would do us all in."

"Yes, enough to take in, that's for sure." Talandat stood up and began to pace, then sat back down and looked intently at his long time friend. "What do you suggest now?"

"I suggest another competition between the Tureg and the Candela. We can finally put to rest the jealousy and mistrust. The star can be named any way the discoverer wishes. All bets are off as they should have been back then."

"I sincerely hope they were surprised that antrei were being used for the good of the seamless universe, and not in some kind of Candela hunt."

"To say the least. Some actually began shouting we should just give them to you. That was good to hear. Others were quick to point out that Candela were hurt or had died."

"I don't think that Detention is a good enough punishment for some of our Tureg. They can be pretty quick with their fists."

"Yes. Still it's good that now the Candela know about Detention and that Tureg are punished."

Talandat pushed himself from the boulder and brushed off his robes. He looked steadily at Magistrel and said, "I guess it's my turn now. There are a few Tureg ready to come back from Detention so I will wait until then. And yes, why don't we plan a competition to heal the feud between our two fey—what do you say?"

Magistrel stood up, too, and a slow smile spread across his face. "A friendly competition on neutral grounds to bring our two fey together. To top it off, we could observe Andrielle and Bret."

"Oh yes, I'd forgotten about them. You're right."

"This is going to be even better than I expected."

"It's a grand idea. Let's do it."

Talandat's hand went over to Magistrel's which had come up to meet Talandat's.

"For the good of the seamless universe."

"For the good of the seamless universe, indeed."

"What are they waiting for?" Zac had spent the last few minutes tying and retying his robe. "I thought we'd be back home by now."

"Have no idea," said Bret. He, too, wondered about the delay. However, as he looked around, he noted that Gerhardt was not in the group to be released. Nor was Cancret. He saw that Wyatt and Trent stood close by not exactly ill at ease, but he could tell they were itching to go. All kinds of colors and numbers were finally swirling in bountiful release having been suppressed for their time in Detention. His own, too, were spiraling happily as if he were a new changeling and not yet in control. He never knew how miserable it was to have color denied from spiral or numbers from flash. What a relief.

Cam was slowly approaching in his almost comical feathery waddle. His numerous yellow appendages jauntily flapped when he wanted to join in a conversation. Cam looked for all the garden like tumbleweed out in the desert except that Bret knew first hand how swift Cam could move to stop a fight. Maybe they fabricated this slow sashay as a type of camouflage.

Cam looked at the small group and said, "Fellow travelers in our depths, I give you farewell. For all that you have done to relieve yourselves of ignorance, I salute you. You must keep the seamless universe in balance. That is our only purpose here in the garden."

Finally Cancret and Gerhardt were visible, moving aside the luminous screens that provided both light and parameters to Detention. The two still looked surly. Bret wondered what they'd managed to learn here.

With the entire group convened, colors spiraled up and then together. Numbers were skipping around the small group of Tureg and finally merged into a stream of infinite numbers. Bret closed his eyes and felt for the first time since he came here the sweet touch of prairie smoke tendrils. It was a sure indication that the time in Detention was now complete, and they were going home.

Selat was sitting at their table working sweet grass into long bundles. Bundles like this made strong and sturdy sleeping mats, or baskets, or in this case serving plates. Selat used his fey knife to first make long braids, then shape each into circles. One circle spiraled around another until finally the whole was shaped into a round and large enough flat plate. Sulpicett sat at the table pouring ginger tea into two cups, one for her and one for Jondett. They'd been talking about Bret and the preparations needed for their pairing announcements. There was so much to do and so little time to do it all. Besides, no one knew when Bret was coming back from Detention. There might not even be time to have a pairing announcement party.

A sudden flash of bright light burning as blue as the hottest part of a flame illuminated the entire kitchen. Selat knew what it meant: it was Bret, released from Detention. He stood up smiling and his son appeared after the burning flame wound down. His wife was crying. Jondett beamed and caught up Bret in an embrace that meant the world to him. She was true to her word. They would make a fine pair.

Bret's brother Colt and their sister Margaret came into the kitchen and looked wildly around to see what all the commotion was about. The two finally realized that it was Bret in the middle of the flame although Margaret as the youngest would always claim she saw him first and jumped on top of him.

What a tumble of Tureg – laughing and crying at the same time.

When the call for Assembly went out, the family was ready to face the entire Tureg fey community. Detention terms were over, thank the seamless universe, and the fey were ready to resume their mission with renewed vigor. No one was happier than Bret and Jondett.

PART TWO
The Competition

~ Chapter 9 ~

The hummingbird wove its quick way into the upper garden where it knew the portal of the Candela to be. It had brought messages from Candela out in the field to the home portal whenever they needed service. A Candela intoning the right music called upon it now and then. The music sounded much like the tone produced when it and its flying brothers flicked their wings and flew from one blossom to another. So, when it was hovering over the bee balm in the middle of a valley and heard a song, different from the Candela but just as purposeful, it was surprised to see that a Tureg had originated this call. The Tureg was elderly with a waving beard nearly down to the ground. Must have been some kind of a leader. A message was written on a large inner shard of oak leaf hydrangea bark. The hummingbird flew right away to the portal under the Vanderwolf pine and dropped the message under the chanterelle where it sank down into the brown rich humus.

The Candela council were mystified when the communication came in. The contents of the message spread by word of mouth through the entire cavern at sonic speed. Candela were invited to participate in a competition with the Tureg in the sweet grass field! What in the garden did that mean? Quinn nodded and smiled. Brian was a study in pensiveness as was Amanda. Bruce appeared exasperated, as he threw up his hands. As for Magistrel, he looked like he knew something, as usual.

The Tureg and the Candela were enemies. The reason, yes, had now been revealed. Yet, to think of being in the presence of the enemy was something no Candela could conceive. Outrage could turn to murderous rage in a heartbeat. Hardly any Candela could trust themselves to be within a reasonable distance of a Tureg. Magistrel had to explain things at next Gathering. Until then shock reverberated throughout the cavern.

Later that day Magistrel stood before Gathering spiraling magnesium white and orange striped with flame blue. These colors preempted all others. His voice thundered, "Dear Candela, please consider this. That the Tureg have come to an accommodation of sorts with themselves and when they think of us it is to remember before. What it was like to live in harmony with each other. Let us try also to find a way now that we have been invited to convene with them on a friendly basis. Let's participate in the competition in true Candela spirit."

Bruce stood up and spiraled his colors. Magistrel nodded to him to speak.

"Magistrel, how is it that we can even contemplate a time when we would be alone on the field with the Tureg. Remember our beloved dead Candela who sacrificed their lives observing the garden, as is our mission. How dare you entertain a diplomatic meeting that is designed to put aside our differences? How do you know that the Tureg will keep their side of the bargain? How do you know that the Tureg aren't contemplating killing all of us, cutting off our wings, and, and, and..." Bruce spiraled a large cone of magenta and yellow, signifying outrage and anger.

"You're right – as we are now, we can only suffer, become more outraged—justifiably! —and garner what we can of changelings. We aren't part of that process except through our ignorance. I'm suggesting that this invitation is to take back our responsibility to full measure. My dear Candela, open your hearts. Don't any of you wish this feud to stop? Don't any of you wish to live in peace once more?"

Many of the Candela looked at each other sheepishly and shrugged and waved pastel colors indicating misgivings over aggression, a thinking-it-over mode.

After Gathering, Andrielle and her family convened at their table. The table was laden with a fey meal: dogwood berries, juniper quiche, roquette pine nut salad, and Artemisia tonic. Gwen stood at her end of the table and gestured to Julianna to begin passing around the sumac scones. Cantrel intoned the missive blessing for the family, the fey and the garden.

Andrielle knew it was only a matter of time before the family would judge how they could take part in the competition. It was a dreadful thought that she would have to see that Tureg who'd been there at her injury although she knew in her heart that he hadn't caused it, not really. She wondered what he looked like and what he had been thinking at the time. She remembered the odd feeling of lamb's wool on her shoulders that she'd felt at the time. What a mystery this was. All she really wanted to do was her mission in the garden, which was protecting the balance of the seamless universe. Was that really the mission of the Tureg as well? How can we tell, she thought?

~ Chapter 10 ~

Talandat waved aside all colors and numbers vying for attention and spoke to the Tureg community in Assembly. He also ignored the silent jabs to his mid section as one Tureg after another tried to catch his attention.

"My dear Tureg, now that our imprisoned fey have been returned to us with full rights and responsibilities, it is time for all of you to hear me out on something that will change everything. I have long waited for this to happen and now that our Detention Tureg have come into our midst once more, I have a wonderful announcement to make.

"The Candela have accepted an invitation to a competition in the sweet grass field, as of days of old." Talandat was prepared for outbursts of color and numbers but the sharp edges and rocky terrain rolling about were so robust that they would have knocked him down if the Tureg council members hadn't grabbed him and each other. He didn't know how the council managed standing. Many of the Tureg were rolling about on the cavern's floor reeling as if ocean waves were tumbling them onto sea-wracked shores.

"Are you crazy?" "They couldn't possibly...." "Wait till I get ahold of them this time!" "It's what I've been waiting for – those wings will make fine trophies!" Talandat and his council combined efforts to calm the crowd down with a feeling of soft goose down feathers to cause comfort and warmth up and down the gathered Tureg. Everet even came out from his portal keeper's cubbyhole and viewed the crowd with horror. Talandat was glad to see that he, too, had simmered down.

"Tureg and Talandat," began Everet. "When I saw the hummingbird weaving to our portal I knew something was up. The message it brought was from a Candela."

Talandat said, "It falls to me to explain this to you so please calm down and sit by your numbers. Use the feelings of your family to try and control your color and numbers, and jabs, too. You all look like a bunch of new changelings trying things out. Take care that you do not end up going to the healer."

The Tureg around Bret's family began asking a myriad of questions of each other. Selat looked worried, Sulpicett in shock, Colt looked furious, and Margaret horrified. Bret alone remained calm and caught the eye of Zac, Wyatt and Trent where they were gathered with their families. Each of them knew what Talandat was going to relate. Each of them also figured that Cancret and Gerhardt were going to somehow be trouble.

Deep underneath the ocean crust, deep within the garden's mantle, a meeting of another sort was taking place. Colandid stepped into a lofty meeting area and began calling the rest of his

Dantorak. There were streaks of gold and silver in the solid rock beside swift waterfalls of oil and water that ran straight down from all sides of the cavern. The intermittently spaced waterfalls made a kaleidoscope of sight and sound. Everything solid shimmered from glistening mica. Dantorak were appearing, stepping into the cavern from cracks in the solid rock. Colandid saw that they were all there and began.

"My loyal Dantorak. Thank you for your presence. The last time I noted what the Tureg and Candela were doing, I could sense a conspiracy brewing between them. I think they want to have peace again. On the one hand cooperation between those two is helpful to the garden. But what if, just like usual, it's not. My loyal Dantorak." Colandid looked from one to another of the council. His body robe was covered with amethyst crystals and gold leaf.

Colandid stood before the Dantorak fey proud and pale. He shook his robes and they chimed as the amethyst crystals pinged off each other. Their community of fey had lived their entire existence deep within the center of this garden ever since it sprang from the firmament. They were convinced that their mission had an enormous impact on the garden and kept the seamless universe in balance. They were the true guardians, prepared to do whatever it took to keep this garden pristine and intact. The seamless universe would be better off if all humans were gone. Even better if all other fey were gone, too. It was with regret that the Dantorak did what they did but it had to be done. Regret was one thing, the seamless universe another. And the humans did so little that was worthwhile. In fact, it was humans who decimated the beautiful garden by carving out trenches and grabbing up minerals or dumping waste in the clear water. They initiated all kinds of new bacteria and created virus after virus. So many species extinct before their time. What a waste.

This conspiracy between Tureg and Candela to help humans was becoming intolerable and more so now that those two were becoming friendly to each other again. Oh, the forsaken universe.

His two Dantorak council members sat on quartz crystals near the edge of the clear space. Colandid knew they would have an opinion. Jalenkad was as pale as Colandid. His robes glistened brilliantly with flecks of platinum. "I'm willing to let them attempt it. It may mean that they will come to their senses afterwards. I'm willing to let them attempt it."

The other Dantorak on the council, Koyandel, alluded the same, "We must trust in the seamless universe. There is a reason that the Tureg and Candela exist, we can't just catapult each and every one of them off the garden, much as we'd like to. Maybe the garden is better off with them than without them. After all, we can control them to a great extent. We must trust in the seamless universe." Koyandel was a softie, Colandid thought, but the reasoning did sound solid. The seamless universe was as mysterious as it was beautiful. Oh, for the forsaken universe.

"Ok, but just so they know we're watching, I'm going to allow some mild tremors in their caverns. Just so they know we're watching."

Bret sensed it before it happened. Earthquake tremors began to shake the knobbed chair in the center of the Tureg cavern. It was so sudden no one could fly up fast enough to avoid the aftermath. He was able to grab his little sister Margaret to keep her from falling over. Talandat took hold of the number he was flashing. All the Tureg were either tumbling over or holding onto one another. The silk coverings on compartments wrenched and fell. Sweet grass baskets bounced. Bret knew that Talandat would have something to say about this. He caught the eye of Zac. There were other Tureg, Bret knew, who had been in Detention, and those Tureg were no doubt thinking the same thing: the Dantorak were at it again. Since he'd been in Detention, his attitude had shifted from 'What was that?' to 'What are the Dantorak up to?' This was different. Their whole fey could have been damaged. Why were the Dantorak doing this?

The very same thing was happening in the Candela cavern. The tremors came so fast no Candela was prepared. No one was able to fly away. Andrielle did feel a shiver in her wing tissues some time before her sisters did. She looked up at Magistrel and saw that he was gazing about as if querying the very air. The ground under her feet started to shift and turn. She grabbed her mother and her brother and held onto both of them. She knew that sometimes the garden just did this, but this felt different. There was more rumbling, there were more cracks in the cavern walls. How horrible to see this. Then, to see Bruce sink into a crack in the cavern's floor.

Trumpet blasts and screeches made hearing difficult. Andrielle climbed out from the pile of sweet grass mats that had fallen on top of her. Thank the seamless universe her wings had not been hurt. Looking around the gathering space she noted Candela were pulling themselves out of piles of dogwood berries, pine nuts, and sumac

cones, all of which had fallen down from the compartments surrounding the gathering space. What a mess. Justinda would be in
big demand. She saw Magistrel and the rest of the council off to one
side speaking in low tones and then Magistrel flew up and off.

Tureg had tumbled everywhere and Bret's family were brushing
themselves off, picking up the jumbled and tossed pieces of their cavern. The swirls of color and flashes of numbers were chaotic. What
damage was done remained to be seen, but as Bret looked around,
he saw Cancret and Colandat conferring with Talandat. Probably
trying to convince Talandat that they needed to go out and beat up a
few Candela for surely they'd done something to cause the Dantorak
to retaliate against the garden like this.

Talandat put a hand on each of their shoulders and they looked
chagrinned. Then Talandat called for order and began to speak.

"My dear Tureg, this is exactly what I'm talking about—the garden might be in jeopardy. Did someone go and see how the nursery
is? Some of you better go see how the people are doing, too. There
might be more catastrophes in store for us. I must go off and meet
with Magistrel, the Regent of the Candela. A truce between us is
now mandatory. We must have peace, or all might be lost." Talandat
took off and left the rest of the Tureg to put the cavern to rights.

~ Chapter 11 ~

Where am I, was the first thought Bruce had when he came to. He remembered falling, or maybe being drawn down into the crack that formed right under his feet. He remembered seeing baskets of acorns and sweet grass mats tumbling from compartment after compartment. Things happened so fast that no one was flying anywhere. He was now sprawled in a small cavern filled with lustrous quartz crystals and phosphorescent light.

He looked around and noticed a widening fissure in the cavern wall out of which a very pale creature floated. The robe the creature wore was embedded with gold flecks and amethyst crystals. Bruce knew it was fey, yet one he'd never seen before.

The fey sat down on a large quartz crystal and Bruce was surprised that he could understand anything he said, because it was not audible in the ordinary sense. This fey was more than unusual.

"I brought you here for a good reason," Bruce heard in his mind. "I wanted to talk with one of you Candela. Very beautiful wings, by the way." Bruce pulled his wings back closer into his body. "As you can see, I have no wings, but believe me, I can fly. There's no need to worry for the time being. I brought you here for a good reason."

"Are you keeping me prisoner? Will I go back to my cavern?" Bruce asked. "You must know that I am not without influence in my fey. I am part of our governing council and when Magistrel hears ......"

"Most surely you will go back to your cavern," the pale creature said. "I would like you to take a message to Magistrel from me. My name is Colandid, the Regent of the Dantorak. I know all about the feud between you Candela and the Tureg. I was glad that the two of you came to such a disagreement. The garden would be better off without any of you. By the way, you Candela have been incredibly short-sighted. So, I will be watching closely to see how your competition turns out. The Candela and the Tureg must come to their senses. If you agree to bring this message back, most surely you will go back to your cavern." Bruce noted with amusement the doubling up Colandid did with his speech.

"What difference does it make to you? Sir, I have no love for the Tureg, they've done damage to our fey time and again, but we have a good chance to repair things between the two of us, and maybe just maybe that will do this garden some good in the end." Bruce stood up tall and wrapped his robe around himself in defiance.

"This makes a great deal of difference to me and my kind. If it weren't for you and the Tureg, this garden would be in pristine condition. It's because of you that humans thrive. Humans thoughtlessly damage the four elements, and there's no end of that in sight. This makes a great deal of difference to me and my kind."

"If you know so much, you know that we rescue ephemerals from the humans and give them another purpose. How does that not help the garden and the seamless universe?"

"We know all about your rescues. And here's another thing. If you and the Tureg make peace, we will be watching very carefully so that the seamless universe is not bothered by anything you try to do to help humans. We know all about your rescues."

It was a warning, from an enigma.

Bruce was not a big fan of the Tureg, but he was now more determined than ever to work with them to stop these ominous Dantorak. How dare they? Who were they to demean the people in the garden? What was the Dantorak's true mission? Bruce could only think that they wanted to be the only fey in this garden. And they weren't going to stop until they were.

Both Talandat and Magistrel looked disheveled when they met at the red rock boulder. The sweet grass waved high and bright green.

"Can you believe what just happened – how are the Tureg?" Magistrel gazed at his old friend and saw that he, too, was as grim as himself.

"We're all fine, Magistrel, and I trust you all are, too. Barring a few strains and bruises. It's strange that there weren't any worse injuries. Still I wish it hadn't happened." Talandat began pacing around the boulder. "You know, this might have been a warning, a message from the Dantorak. It could be they are worried that we'll start getting along again." Talandat stopped and gazed at his friend, who by this time had sat down with his chin resting on his fist, his elbow on his knee.

"I know what you mean. But we lost a Candela – Bruce fell through a crack in the cavern floor."

"Pine nuts to dogwood, you'll hear from him again. And he'll bring a message from the Dantorak. By the seamless universe, it's time for real action. Magistrel, we've finally decided to have the competition again. Let's make it a real healing gift to each other."

"Yes, shall we have the planning committee meet here, as in the old days?"

"Right here, how about later on today?"

"I'll alert my council. Let's get it started. By the seamless universe!"

In the Candela cavern, Magistrel found his council gathered at the knobbed root table and was glad to see that Bruce had indeed returned.

"Where were you?"

"What happened?"

"How did you get back?"

"Tell us all about it!"

All the council were both happy and mystified to see Bruce. He looked well although disheveled, as they all did.

"You can't believe where I've been. Magistrel, isn't there something you need to tell us all? You know, about the third faction of fey in our garden?" Bruce looked knowingly at Magistrel, who had the good grace to look a bit sheepish. The stunned looks on the council's faces were in severe contrast to Quinn's resigned look.

"It's true, my dear council, that yes, I've kept the existence of the Dantorak from you. Only those fey who go back to the time of the firmament know about them. But again, it's time to reveal that as well."

"There's been too much secretiveness for too long, don't you think?" Again, Bruce looked knowingly at the leader of the Candela.

"Yes, it seemed wiser to let things settle. Bruce, perhaps you could start by giving us a report?"

"Well, I was drawn down into some kind of cavern. There were fey there, the Dantorak, they called themselves. These fey don't have wings although they say they fly. I didn't see anyone fly. I stood there and these shapes floated out of a crack alongside a quartz wall where a waterfall of oil fell. They spoke to me without speaking out loud. I heard them in my mind. That was another strange thing. They were very clear that I was there to bring back a message. Their leader Colandid was right smart about it too. He said, and I quote: 'If you and the Tureg make peace, we will be watching very carefully so that the seamless universe is not bothered by anything you try to do to help humans.' Magistrel, I don't trust them. I think they want us to stay at war with the Tureg. That way, the Dantorak can keep on disrupting the garden at will. I don't like them at all. What do you know about them – what can you tell us?"

Magistrel looked concerned as he began to tell his council about the Dantorak.

"They also sprang from the first child's laugh at the beginning, just like us. They also have missions of contributing to the garden, and protecting the balances in the seamless universe. With a difference. The Dantorak began to believe that the garden would be better off without people. It is humanity, after all, that impose imbalances of enormous consequence. We try to heal those imbalances, as part of our mission. Over time, the Dantorak began to believe that the balance of the seamless universe would be better accomplished by thwarting the humans, so they withdrew their communication with us and from the Tureg, too."

"It was strange beyond what I've ever encountered—what that leader Colandid said, and how he said it. As if they were just going to wait at the sidelines and then swoop in when the Candela and Tureg were least suspecting. Whatever happens, we have to be careful where they are concerned. They don't want people in the garden."

Amanda looked startled as she said, "Maybe they're to blame for the lack of Candela changelings. Do you think that they take ephemerals? Or somehow our own changelings are captured by them?"

Magistrel said, "No, they increase their number by collapsing a human at will. They don't bother with our ephemerals or changelings at all. But the danger there is that they could take all the humans."

Quinn spoke the words all were thinking, "If the Dantorak don't want humans to exist, how would they replenish their own numbers? For that matter, would any of us exist if there were no humans? They're crazy! The first of any of us fey came from the first laugh of the first child, for the sake of the seamless universe."

Amanda added, "This is so much to take in. Have the Dantorak forgotten how we all came to be?"

"There's no telling what's going on in their minds. Once they severed all communication with the Candela and the Tureg, their whole outlook on humans and fey must have changed, but we really don't know. It's probably good that they've made contact through Bruce. Perhaps in the end we will all come together like it was at the beginning, for the benefit of all of us in the garden."

The entire council were a study in introspection as they pondered what Magistrel said next. "We'd better take care of first things first: working again with the Tureg, and then trying to see how to deal with the Dantorak."

~ Chapter 12 ~

Magistrel sat on his chair next to the Candela knobbed root table and contemplated his council. He knew they were of good heart, as filled with the mission of the Candela as ever.

Quinn began as an ephemeral from a live baby whose parents so greatly loved her as she expired from a fatal defective heart that the fey decided to continue with her name. It was common knowledge that if the original parents' love was noted, the gift of original name could be bestowed on the changeling. There was a note on the blanket gathered around her as she lay in the sweet grass field, that said her name was Quinn. Original name wasn't always bestowed, but such is the way of the mysterious seamless universe.

Magistrel remembered finding her in the sweet grass field, and bringing her into the Candela cavern when he was still in the mission of finding changelings. He and his wife Colima thought they would be gifted with her only because they felt so captivated by her. His existence went back to the time of the firmament so he thought it was possible, but Quinn went to another couple. He felt like all sorrowful fey who did not have a changeling. In time he saw that Quinn was well loved, was beautifully prized, and that was satisfying after a while. He and Colima were given changelings as time went on. They could be involved in Quinn's life in ways other than parenting her. Quinn's fey parents sadly expired by the beaks of an osprey and a turkey vulture when Quinn had grown to full fey. How wonderful to see that her grit and intelligence was so keen that she was part of his council. He mentored her and saw with pride that she flourished. He now sought her counsel.

Magistrel saw that Brian, Bruce and Amanda were looking to him for his counsel. Brian favored finding a way that Candela could gather ephemerals. Bruce was opposed to any connection to the Tureg simply because there were so many unresolved problems between them. Like the beatings and the torn and useless wings that resulted. Near and actual deaths of Candela. Magistrel knew Amanda was trying to do her best to figure out what was the right course of action for the Candela. She desperately thought about the future of Candela changelings.

"My dear Candela," Magistrel looked at each of them tenderly. "Talandat and I have met and decided that it's best that the competition go forward as soon as possible. The earthquake did minimal damage to our two caverns. From the message that Bruce brought us, it's possible the Dantorak want the Candela and the Tureg to remain enemies. That somehow it's beneficial that we are busy fighting each other."

"And so we should. They're our first enemy. Let's put them in their place, and then deal with these Dantorak fey." Bruce was earnest in his desire to help his fey, Magistrel knew. "On the other hand, if it's true that our real enemy is the Dantorak, then we need to have a truce with the Tureg. I don't like it much but such is the seamless universe. I'll try to put my dislike aside for the good of our fey."

Magistrel smiled. Bruce usually convinced himself after first being righteously angry. Good. Now for the rest. They sat looking at him with near perfect concentration. What they decided would have far reaching effects.

Quinn was the next to speak. "My fellow council elders, we have to realize that we would not exist without the Tureg transforming ephemerals, and giving Candela changelings to us. I'm ashamed that we've been at war with them. It's awful. What they must think of us. Withholding our antrei when it's so easy for us to pick up our sloughed-off ones and set them aside for the Tureg. I say, let's do it, let's work with them. Let's show the seamless universe that even though this thing has blown so out of proportion, we know how to take the first step. Magistrel, I'd be happy to be part of the group to organize the competition."

Again Magistrel smiled. Quinn did make a fine leader.

Brian spiraled a brilliant yellow striped with deep pink. "Maybe contact with the Tureg is OK. Maybe we could find out how to gather our own ephemerals. If the Tureg can do it, maybe, just maybe, we could find a way. Then we wouldn't have to depend on them so much. I don't know. I'm confused. They've been giving us our changelings all along, even as we've done everything we can to avoid them. Shame on us. I think that Quinn's advice is exactly right. We need to plan a competition. I'd be willing to be part of the planning, too."

Amanda was last to speak, and was shaking her head. "All this time," she said, "all this wasted time. How could we be so selfish, and not see that our changelings rose and fluctuated in numbers as the seamless universe designs. Not how we would have it be. We have a lot to apologize for. I hope the Tureg will listen. I, too, would like to be part of the planning."

Magistrel nearly glowed silvery white, as brilliant as the undersides of clouds covering the sun. "I knew you all would do the right thing. Candela and Tureg councils will plan this competition. We need to do this soon, before the next harvest, which is very close by the looks of the sweet grass field. We shall announce the competition at Gathering and then the council will fly to confer with the Tureg. Barring any more earthquakes that is!" A bit of humor to lighten the mood, not that it really did.

Telling the Candela about the Dantorak at Gathering had gone as well as could be expected. The Candela had heard one shock after the other. First about the ephemerals, then the reasons for the ongoing war with the Tureg, and now about this third fey community, the Dantorak. What in the garden did it all mean? Were there more fey out there? Were all of them evil? Candela color and music explosions had been played out so much lately that there wasn't much in the seamless universe that was going to shake them again. There was a certain amount of resignation in the colors bouncing around, and the sounds were more like an orchestra tuning up than anything worse. Well, Magistrel did learn that everyone tasted rancid mushroom stew, which sounded about right. The Dantorak had been an unknown so far in the Candela cavern, and hopefully collaboration between the Tureg and Candela might mean an easier time dealing with them.

Following Gathering, the garden took on the look and feel of a perfect late summer day. The Candela council flew off in concert to the sweet grass field, the mellow middle A note humming around them, and the swirl of rainbow spectrum reflected in the antrei of their wings. Hummingbirds and ducks accompanied them in an attempt to shield them from patrolling raptors. And that did the job. The group flew in relative safety.

Talandat and his council waited for them with green and blue numbers shifting, adding, expostulating, resolving. Shalik and Robert flanked him. Thaddeus and Corat sat on sweet grass bundles. Talandat knew his council had hoped for this meeting for a long time. Their council meeting had gone well, too. They were aggrieved over the offenses they'd committed in retrieving antrei, and hopeful that their problems could be smoothed over. Behind them were a number of gifts for the Candela: sweet grass baskets, acorns, and vats of juniper and gooseberry tonic. These things took time to craft and accumulate. And best of all, they had a huge vat of saffron-edelweiss infused honey, the very honey that was the tipping point in the feud between the Candela and the Tureg.

As the Candela landed near the red rock boulder striped with basalt and quartz crystals, they all stood up. Magistrel and Talandat embraced. The two councils looked both wary and curious. The trouble between both fey happened long before any of their ephemerals had been rescued.

"Magistrel, these Tureg fey are my council members: Shalik, my pair, whom you met long ago."

Magistrel approached the beautiful Tureg, bowed, took her hand and kissed it. "I'm so glad we meet again. Your conversation has been something my pair Colima and I have truly missed."

"And I, too, Magistrel. Please give Colima my greetings."

"I'd like to introduce Robert of our council." Robert approached Magistrel and shook his hand reverently, looking as seriously grim as all the rest of the Tureg council.

"Thaddeus and Corat are our youngest council members." Corat gazed into Magistrel's face as if looking for the answers to unanswerable questions. Thaddeus shifted a bit from foot to foot, as serious as they all were.

Talandat then was introduced to the Candela council, and saw them flinch as he approached. "We are here, dear fey, to put to rest our differences. Do not fear our Tureg or me. We are not here to steal your antrei, we are here to apologize for our selfishness."

"It's us that were selfish," Amanda's eyes filled with tears that threatened to spill over. She blinked them back. "So much wasted energy and time." She firmly lifted her chin, straightened up and took the few steps toward Shalik with a bundle wrapped in a shimmering cloth. As Shalik unwrapped it, Talandat knew all would be well. Five antrei of aurora borealis coloration were nestled together. "I've gathered these up, and it's time to give them to you. Please accept them with my and our thanks." Amanda stepped back into the first yellow and blue spiral of the meeting and all watched as the two colors, one of the warm spectrum and one of the cool spectrum, melded and blended into the green of the balanced universe.

Talandat and Magistrel began the meeting between the two fey councils with a ritual cup of juniper tonic, and pine nut sumac nectar scones. Afterwards, they sipped dandelion and sorrel tea. When all were refreshed and rested, Talandat began.

"Let me explain how a competition is run. Magistrel and I lived during much happier times. That was when Tureg and Candela joined in friendship and full purpose, and it was considered worthy to have an assembly of our two fey where more of the unique missions of the fey could be pursued. The Dantorak by this time were keeping to themselves, but we knew they were watching all the same. Our competition was held after harvesting sweet grass and there was much celebration, and feasting. A competition in the strictest of senses may mean that one has to win out and one has to lose. But in our competitions what was thought worthy was what was created for the garden. As I recall, we had several categories. One was to see who could find something new: a new color, a new star, a different sweep of the wind, a new species of fish or animal, or wildflower. Another use for wild forage. Then there was the competition of devising: devise a an alarm system to catch a lie; devise a method for discerning a human's true wishes; devise a method to calculate the depth of the ocean, or the distance of the stars."

Magistrel cleared his throat. "There was also, as I recall, the weaving competition: weave a dream; weave the aurora borealis into cloth; weave a basket that never is empty; weave a tapestry that reveals the future; weave a landscape: a pond, a forest glade, a brook; weave with the warp of truth and the weft of speculation; weave a fishnet that catches a dream."

Talandat added, "There was carving. Carve the hopes of birds; carve the gentility of ivory; carve the way we see beauty; carve the way we discern love."

"How did one win a competition, and what did they win?" Thaddeus, as intrigued as all were, spoke the question hanging in the air.

Magistrel and Talandat looked at each other and in spite of themselves started to laugh.

"Talandat, do you still have your clear gold chain?"

"Oh my garden, it's one of my treasures. This is a clear gold chain from which hangs a moonstone circular amulet. When I put it up to my ear, I can hear star-song, the music of whirling stars."

Shalik spoke, "And I love the way it looks around my neck, too."

Everyone laughed. Thaddeus asked, "Was that a prize? What kind of competition was that?"

Talandat explained. "That was a task that definitely made me think. I was to position myself in the upper atmosphere, catching sparks as I could from meteors, plus all the silver shine from the undersides of clouds, and reflections from the moon on the ocean's waves. All to find a way to harness star beams that fall to the garden during cloudless nights. Then, I had to encapsulate that light into a crystal. That was hard. I went through the usual minerals, and came to moonstone by accident. It worked because the crystal is a wonderful receptor for light. From then on, all moonstone has glowed, so the seamless universe was enhanced, humans and fey were benefited. A by-product is the fact that one can hear the star song. I don't really know how that happened, but that's the way it works."

"So why did you get to keep it?"

Magistrel said, "In those days, when a fey completed a task, sometimes what was produced could be given to one fey. A clear gold chain with a moonstone amulet is a good example. In the case of something with a larger purpose, both Tureg and Candela would jointly share. Like a new wildflower, or another octave of music."

Corat cleared her throat, waited a minute before speaking. "It sounds as if fey competitions are truly different from human competitions. In theirs, people somehow are pitted one to one—someone wins, someone loses. Our 'winning' is misnamed—perhaps we should change that to mean accomplished or realized."

That would be the first of many questions that needed to be answered. Magistrel asked Talandat how he wanted to proceed. The competition's guidelines needed to be revamped, all of them knew that, and there were many issues to cover. Should they take into consideration the different missions of the two fey? Should they have different categories for each fey, or find some comparable tasks for both fey, given their unique sensations? They were starting at ground zero, and the main idea was to bring Tureg and Candela together. Could they really accomplish that?

Magistrel and Talandat asked for suggestions. Thaddeus and Corat both spiraled colors.

Thaddeus spoke, "We've been talking among ourselves ever since Talandat explained in Assembly. Both Corat and I believe that it would be wonderful if we termed this a gala Celebration of reuniting our two fey, rather than call it a competition. I know that it's just semantics, just words, but after all, let's grab onto any edge we can."

Amanda asked, "What do you mean when you say Assembly?"

"It's our word for when our whole fey meet to discuss things. What do you call it?"

"We call it 'Gathering.'" Thaddeus and Amanda had found a friendly face in each other.

Both councils began nodding yes and Magistrel was pleased to see it.

"Talandat, my very thinking as well. A competition between brothers and sisters can be harmful if not done with the right mind-set. Let's cut through that. Instead of individuals competing, let's compose our teams of one Tureg and one Candela each. How does that sound to you?"

"That's revolutionary, to say the least," Bruce blared elephant trumpets and spiraled chartreuse from surprise. "On the one hand, we have fey who have been enemies for millennia agreeing to meet on a neutral field. On top of that, they actually must suspend animosity and work together." He brightened up somewhat, and the chartreuse began to sparkle with a deepening golden orange. "You know, it might make battlefield friendships. On the other hand, if we continue to separate our two fey, justified animosities and suspicions will deepen. Well, working together as teams may just work!" Magistrel was glad that Bruce spelled it out. His confusion mirrored all present, but they all knew they had to make it work.

Robert spoke up. "It could be that our different approaches can be combined. Tureg spiral numbers and color, and then experience a physical reaction."

Quinn asked, "What do you mean ... like sneezing?"

"Not exactly. Let me explain. When I'm near my friends or family, I may feel a silk scarf on my shoulders. Something pleasant. When I'm near an enemy, it's pokes and jabs, sometimes quite severe. And Candela ... excuse me, how would you explain it?"

Amanda said, "We spiral music and color. Beautiful lyrical music when things are going well, and then raucous clanging when things are bad. Also, the same thing can be said of Candela tasting things when we aren't eating or drinking anything. Good or rotten tastes, depending. How can our different perceptions be combined?"

"I know that when I encounter or sense something unpleasant, I have an awful taste in my mouth, like bitter tansy for instance," said Quinn. "Good tastes come when I meet with friends, family, or something wonderful happens. It tastes like juniper compote, or the first raspberries plucked in spring."

Robert was next. "Something tough, like hearing about the Candela, becomes rocky terrain, or punches and kicks that end up giving us bruises. A pleasant experience becomes lambs' wool floating onto my shoulders, or friendly backslaps like when my friends and I gather at the edge of a brook in the moonlight." All the Candela threw Robert a surprised look.

Magistrel explained. "Let's not worry here about our differences, but concentrate on our similarities. We all have families, we all have friends, and we all care about the seamless universe and the garden." He gazed about at his Candela meaningfully.

Robert said, "By composing our teams of one Tureg and one Candela, we might indeed come up with very unusual winning combinations for the competition. Well, I mean the Celebration."

"And that will emphasize our desire to heal the rift between our two fey." Talandat began his pacing again. Magistrel sat with his chin balanced on his fist.

The looks of all fey present were a sight to see. Determined smiles like flashes of colorful brilliance appeared all around.

~ Chapter 13 ~

The entire Tureg community was silent when Talandat broke the news to them in Assembly: the competition was to go forth, and on top of all that, each team was to be made up of one Tureg and one Candela.

What?

Bret was even more mystified when he saw that he had been teamed up with a female Candela named Andrielle. Was that the Candela he had gone to Detention for? He hadn't shared with Jondett yet that he was on a team with a female from the Candela. Would she mind, really? There was no way he could make it up to the Candela for what he had done, or was thought to have done. In reality he was looking forward to coming face to face with her again. That startling blaze of sunflower yellow continued to haunt him and pop up into his daydreams. He hadn't told Jondett about his daydreams, because instinct told him Jondett might not like to hear that. There was to be a 'meet and greet' for all the Tureg and Candela teams the next day in the sweet grass field. The way Talandat put it was priceless.

"My dear Tureg, it's obvious to you now how important work-ing together with the Candela is going to be, to benefit not only our and their fey, but the entire garden and the seamless universe itself. First off, we are calling this our Celebration, to indicate it's a Celebration of our two fey working cooperatively again. Toward this end, the two councils decided that teams be chosen ahead of time: one Tureg and one Candela to serve on each team. The list is floating around the cavern now. All selected are to go to the sweet grass field tomorrow morning for a meet and greet, where you will meet your Candela teammates. Don't be alarmed that you were not chosen to compete. After all, we need our nursery attendant staff to remain with the ephemerals, and we still have to monitor the garden. However, there will only be a short staff on call tomorrow and during the Celebration itself. I believe this same announcement is going on in the Candela cavern," Talandat looked amused to see the shocked faces of his Tureg.

And then a warning from their Regent. "It goes without saying, that anyone who does not comport themselves respectfully and honorably at this Celebration will be off to Detention immediately." The entire Tureg at Gathering sat subdued and wide-eyed.

"Calm down, everyone!" Magistrel knew that his fey would be somewhat uneasy, but the cacophony of sounds shrieking across the cavern rivaled the time when he spoke to them about the Tureg. The Dantorak they could take since the Dantorak were not exactly a known quantity, but meeting with the Tureg was something no one was going to like much. Bruce stood up and began.

"Now listen up, everyone. I was aghast to learn I had to work with those miserable Tureg. But let's face it. They are not the enemy we think they are. The Dantorak are as horrible as the raptors, and many times more our enemy than the Tureg, believe it or not. The Tureg are so much different than those Dantorak. Tureg are as worried about our existence as we are. They put their anklets on one at a time, just like we do, and they like the same kind of tonic that we do, juniper, wormwood, elderberry. Our garden survives because we actually do work together whether we knew about it or not– they give us our changelings, for the seamless universe's sake. We have to patch things up and this is how it's going to happen, so let's just get used to it."

"I promise you," Magistrel said, "that no one will hurt you, no one will take your wings from you. You yourselves will gather up any of your fallen antrei and you will place them in gathering baskets set around the grounds. So please don't worry for your own safety. The list of teammates is floating around the cavern, so please check and see if your name is on it. Naturally, there will be some of us that stay in the cavern, and those that patrol the garden, but it'll really be only a small staff. I want us all to meet here tomorrow sharply at dawn, so that we can fly en masse to the sweet grass field together."

Andrielle waited until the Candela had cleared out to their compartments for the dinner meal. She told her family she needed to talk with Magistrel. What in the garden did he mean by making her team up with a Tureg? Bret? What kind of a name is that? What if it were the one who had accosted her? Her wings were as good as new, but nothing had really cured her shock. She was even worried about her review classes ending soon. Then she'd have to go out there! She might not be able to control herself, and when she came across a Tureg, she might hurl things at them, hopefully something that would hurt them bad!

"Come here, Andrielle," Magistrel and the rest of his council were still seated at the knobbed table, preparing to leave for their compartments until they noticed she was approaching. "I'm glad to say a few words to you."

"Magistrel, I'm so angry," Andrielle began. "How could I be chosen to participate? I was the last one they hurt. Couldn't I just watch? I need time to get used to the sight of them."

"It's very important that you do compete." Magistrel looked very stern at Andrielle. "You are a role model for all Candela. As the last one accosted, you must show our fey that working together comes first, before our own self-interest. I want you to promise me that you'll put aside your righteous anger against Tureg, so that for the common good of us all, we can actually find a way to co-exist. Can you promise me that?"

Andrielle straightened up. Her Regent had singled her out; she had a duty to perform. "I see what you mean, Magistrel. Yes, I'll swallow my anger. Besides, they don't look any different than we do. It's just that there's no music with them, is there?"

Magistrel said, "Andrielle, you do this, and you won't be disappointed. I know you want to get your pound of flesh, like the people say. You probably will, in the end. Keep an open mind, will you? Consider that you may not want it by then." His kindly smile to her conveyed vast wisdom. Nevertheless, Andrielle thought that was a crazy notion. She sighed and flew to her compartment. On the way she heard her family intoning the key of G signifying the beginning of the evening dance and meal.

The meal would have to wait. The next thing the entire Candela heard was the severe blare of a siren. Three loud bursts and two seconds of silence. Then three more. Oh my garden, Andrielle thought, now we're in for it! The entire Candela emerged from their compartments and converged again around the knobbed table. Magistrel was ready for them.

"My Candela, divide into your squadrons, please, and let's go quickly. There's been a severe earthquake in the part of the garden called Haiti. We have to help the humans there. One squadron look for any people caught or trapped in their homes. One squadron help the animals survive. Another look to help clean up bacteria so fresh clear water is available. You know what to do. One more thing. There will be Tureg there– this time you don't have to waste time hiding from them—do you hear me? See if you can work together on this. Now – take off!"

Bret was searching in the rubble of a collapsed building. He came across a silent baby, who appeared nearly lifeless. The baby was still breathing. Close by were people with long sticks probing the insulation that had exploded out of the walls and roof of the now decimated home. The baby lay in its tiny space. Bret flew to the child and talked into its ear. This prompted the child to cry, which alerted the people. They heard the crying, thank the seamless universe. Bret saw large hands come and lift it up.

He and his squadron saw Candela shoring up roofs so human rescuers could find the trapped people underneath. Then he and several other Tureg helped Candela hold up a heavy beam under a bridge where people were huddled, afraid to step out into the sunlight. They clearly had panicked and were convinced that if they stepped out from under the bridge they'd fall into cracks in the land. Stress made people do the strangest things. Panic, even worse. He looked over at the Candela, and nodded to one. Wary glances went back and forth, but fey hands grasped the underside of the beam, and stabilized it until the people underneath finally left their so-called refuge. As soon as the last person stepped out from under the bridge, the fey let go, and the entire bridge collapsed. People were crying, praying, searching for their families. Fey toiled many hours to help stabilize the area, with the Tureg using the gift of camouflage to help rescue when it proved better to have human hands rather than fey hands.

At the boulder, Talandat was pacing and Magistrel was seated with his chin in his hand.

"Talandat, this is a test, isn't it? The Dantorak are at it again. One disaster after another—right after the oil spill, two earthquakes. By the way, did you know that Candela helped with the oil spill? Pine nuts to dogwood, Candela kept hidden from the Tureg on that mission. However, we alerted the ocean creatures to stay away from the spill – our hummingbirds and ducks helped. They kept the raptors busy, thank the seamless universe, or all of us would have had some casualties."

"I'm thinking that our two fey have learned a great deal by this latest disaster. It'll prove to be good for us, bad for the people, as usual. Sometimes it seems as if fey only benefit when people suffer. It's only through human suffering that we have ephemerals."

Magistrel was a study in contemplation. "Yes, it's a mystery how the seamless universe works. We are benefitting people this time as best we can by rectifying the effects of the earthquake. It was a strong one. What could humanity have done for the Dantorak to take such offense?"

"It's as bad as the last tsunami, or the fires on the prairie. The wildflowers are decimated."

"They should come back. Their seeds are plentiful and can live in miserable burnt out soil until they can grow again."

"Let's not talk about burnt out soil. Those wildfires were terrible this year, what are the Dantorak thinking about? We barely saved half the trees."

"When our squadrons come back, let's relax and meet tomorrow for the start of the Celebration. Tomorrow will be a good day."

"Barring any more so-called natural disasters."

~ Chapter 14 ~

Later that day, the Tureg cavern took on a festive air. Perpetual lights hung as usual from the ceiling and sparkled off of the mica chips embedded in the walls. Today though, there were also rose petals floating in the air, and incense wafted as dried sage and sweet anise slowly burned in alabaster cups. Jondett's parents, Bret's parents, their families and the two young fey slowly revolved around the knobbed chair in the center of the assembly space. Talandat stood to the side with a grin on his face as large as all of the stars. He began the ceremonial speech.

"We are gathered here in this time and space to witness that our two fey, Bret and Jondett, have decided to pair. They have each of their family's consent along with the wondrous consent of the seamless universe." Slowly the revolutions around the knobbed chair picked up speed until the color swirl coalesced into a single color spectrum. At the end of the ceremony there were glasses filled with saffron infused tonic, Edelweiss flowers as garnish.

Talandat finished, "My dear Bret and Jondett, we Tureg look forward to your pairing after harvest with all the joy it will entail. Here is a toast honoring your commitment to the seamless universe: for your happiness always, to your effective pairing, to becoming one, and to one day raising a changeling of your own. Here, here!"

Happy shouts went up from all the balconies surrounding the assembly cavern in the way as of time immemorial that Tureg couples announced their intentions.

The next day, early dawn was a marvel. Autumn sky colors competed with the deep purple of aster, Queen Anne's lacey white, and rich goldenrod blooming in abundance at the edges of the sweet grass field. Both groups of Candela and Tureg had arrived and they eyed each other over the red rock basalt and quartz boulder in the middle of the field. There were tables set up with cucumber water cress morsels, borage flower scones, and water kefir berry drinks flavored with allspice. There wasn't much talking going on. Then, names were called and the individual Tureg and Candela began by introducing themselves to each other.

It was no surprise that the two Regents decided to select Andrielle and Bret as teammates. How better to see what the seamless universe had in store for them. When the Regents announced their names, Bret looked for his teammate and saw Andrielle where she stood apart, waiting for a Tureg to approach her. Her wings were at full attention, and she seemed to keep them close in to her body, as if to say, don't you dare!

"Andrielle, I'm your teammate, Bret."

"You! How can *we* be a team?" Andrielle's shock caused forceful sunbeams to radiate as high as the fronds of waving sweet grass.

Bret knew he had to be quick about it or he'd be pummeled flat. He stepped back fast.

"Can you ever forgive me for your pain? I feel like I caused the harm that I know you suffered in our encounter."

"Since you actually did cause the harm, there's no just *feeling* about it. You are to blame!" Andrielle turned nearly red with explosive music soaring around her. And yet the same feeling of lamb's wool soothed her cheek, so she knew that the Tureg in front of her was telling the truth. Oh, for the sake of the seamless universe.

"I know. I hope you are well or on your way to being well?"

"Almost."

"Tell me about it, I'd really like to know."

"Maybe you should know. First, the gravel cut into my antrei. I lay there beating against the stones, trying to get away from you. That tore me up pretty good. Justinda the Healer gave me some poultice to put on them and they eventually fell off and new ones took their place. Thankfully there were no holes in my wings, but there could have been." Andrielle had begun to shout.

Bret started to cringe a bit at the violence in her voice, but knew he had to endure her words. "Was there anything else?"

"If you mean about the sockets to my wings—YES. One was pulled almost out. I saw you fly away—you could fly! I had to crawl to our cavern. And then I had to take review classes all over again. But the worst was I couldn't fly." Andrielle had started to cry.

"Well, um, I'm glad you can fly again..." Bret was beside himself with remorse. What could he do to ease her pain? What was this? It was surprising to him that he even cared. Yet the sun-drenched yellow flashes she continued to emote had softened to the point that they surrounded him with empathy and the desire to make all her suffering go away. How could this be? He'd just had the pairing announcement last night. Well, this meant nothing, just that he felt some regret. He had to work with her, anyone could see that it was for the greater good of the seamless universe. Jondett would understand, for sure. After all, they were going to be paired tomorrow night, they'd just had their pairing announcement ceremony.

After the meet and greet, as tenuous as oil and water attempting to mix, the Celebration was to begin with each team of Candela and Tureg first harvesting sweet grass.

Talandat cleared his throat and all attention was directed to him. "My dear Candela and my dear Tureg." By the intense looks all around him, Talandat knew he had to find a really good way to begin. "Welcome to the Celebration that both of your Regents have long waited for. Try to contemplate that this is for the good of the seamless universe, for our garden, and for both our fey. By all means be observant for raptors, there are several voles in the area digging in the ground and you know what that means. The ground squirrels are making a racket too. Keep your heads and wings about you. Now, go forth, the seamless universe awaits you." After both Tureg and Candela spent a few minutes looking at each other, a cheer went up. Fey laughter first started tenuously and then, springing forth as joyous as a waterfall.

Gathering up sweet grass was a good first task. Both fey used it to fashion everyday utensils, and weavings for their homes. After that, it would be picking juniper berries and cutting boughs of fragrant wormwood. Harvesting prairie smoke had been considered, but discounted since prairie smoke bloomed and gave out their tendrils in the spring, many months ago. The Tureg had already gathered them, or as least as much as they could, given the wild-fires. Everyone knew that for prairie smoke wildflowers to flourish, they needed the semi dry conditions the wide open prairie afforded. Barring any unforeseen circumstances, the wildflowers would grow back. Next year, when both fey were fully reconciled, the Candela would join in the springtime harvest.

Teams of one Candela and one Tureg stood by uneasily, looking at anything but each other. They'd been chosen as teammates for the duration of the entire Celebration. It was hoped that accomplishing their tasks together would make for better communication between individuals, which would lead to both fey communities finally ending the hostilities.

Bret and Andrielle flew off carrying the large basket between them, his right hand and her left one, into the sweet grass field. Behind them came three other teams. Zac and Pamela was one. Kate and Mitchell, and Daniel and Margaret, were the other two. The four couples made up their harvesting taskforce. Bret and Daniel studied each other before they took off.

"It was you, wasn't it? Don't I remember you from the last disaster?"

Bret answered him, "Yes. You and I held up the bridge together. That was a good job. I'm glad to see you again."

"You know, Andrielle is my sister. So I'll be watching you. Don't try anything funny."

Bret solemnly said back, "I have only the best of intentions toward Andrielle, whatever you think."

"That's right, you do."

"You're teamed with my sister Margaret, so that goes double for you."

"I'm glad we understand each another."

Right, that was settled.

Whatever they gathered would be shared equally. Two elder council fey, one from the Tureg and one from the Candela would oversee the sections, making sure of the count, and the cutting off of the blanched ends. Amanda and Thaddeus were in charge of the section the four teams flew into.

Suddenly Bret's ingrained raptor sensor went on high alert, and he grabbed Andrielle by the arm and tugged her under cover of a low-lying juniper branch. She tried to pull away from him, but then she saw them. In fact, they all saw the dive-bombing falcons, with outstretched claws and open beaks. Everyone scattered. Behind the rocks, into tall clumps, even ducking into the few crevices in the ground. When would the seamless universe make it possible for them to be invisible to the raptors? They heard beaks clicking furiously throughout the wavering strands of sweet grass. The voles in the vicinity did not dive into their holes fast enough, and the fey saw dangling legs quiver as falcons soared up and away. That could have been them.

The fey looked at each other. All knew the danger they were in, day after day. Grim smiles and grim expressions were on all their faces. Another day was theirs.

Andrielle said to Bret as she brushed herself off, "At least you didn't step on my wings this time."

Bret spotted a large clump of sweet grass waving tall and brilliant green. The eight fey circled the clump and lightly landed on the ground. Each stalk had to be gathered individually, leaving the rootstock in place to grow next year. Their hands were just large enough to grasp the stalk as far down as they could, close to the ground. Then with a swift and gentle pull the stalk came loose. The green color that ran the length suddenly blanched very white at the end, which was the part of the stalk that hadn't seen the sun. This was most precious since it made for good eating. Right under the watchful gaze of Amanda and Thaddeus, the teams gulped down the first ones. Such an ambrosia taste, wild and sweet and energizing. The rest were set aside for the feast that evening. Finally Amanda enjoyed a taste, too, as this was her first Celebration. Thaddeus wisely ate some, too, just to join in, and everyone decided to let 'what happens at harvest, stay at harvest.'

They made a good team, Bret and Andrielle, one pulling, one cutting off the blanched ends into a basket and laying the long green stalks in large piles. Brown ends and any dried up wisps were cut away and tossed into a pile for use in the bonfires later on. They kept only the very fresh, those brilliant green stalks that fey prized for craftwork. Eventually, long lanky bundles of sweet grass lay tied along their lengths on the field and were several times the length of the tallest fey. It took all four couples to carry each one back to the boulder for storage and distribution. The boulder area was beginning to look like a city made of green logs and the fragrance held everyone in thrall. The weavers and crafters of this precious commodity were envied.

After the sweet grass harvest the teams flew off to the juniper forest and plucked berries until their bright fragrance made all of them laugh. Wormwood came next, with its intoxication. Several on their team went into the dreamy daze wormwood was known for. At the end of the harvest time, at the end of the day, it seemed that animosity between the team members had almost disappeared. Well, had lessened. It was true that a common goal brought the best out of everyone. The teams left their baskets of sweet grass ends, juniper berries and wormwood boughs by the boulder. Tureg and Candela left to go back to their caverns, to return back within a few hours with offerings for the feast. All seemed to be going well, generally speaking.

~ Chapter 15 ~

As Bret flew back to his cavern, he knew he was still in trouble. After her quick thank you for saving her from the falcons, he thought they were on better terms. So, he'd tried to be friendly to her during the gathering up of sweet grass and juniper berries, but for the most part she was indifferent to him. She let the baskets clump down, as if to say, 'Glad that's over' and swooped away. She had great wings, he couldn't help notice once again.

A gift for her, Bret thought, would make her see he really was sorry. And, he reasoned, it might also help her resign to being teamed with him. After all, it was for the good of the seamless universe, and their councils had chosen them as a team. What in the garden was most desirable, he wondered, that in obtaining one for her would show how sincere he was?

He thought about what Jondett once mentioned she wanted beyond all things, a necklace strung with pearls of pure oxygen. If a fey was honest, all wished to own such a necklace. Even his mother and sister. Harvesting the globes was complicated because the timing had to be just right. Would Andrielle even know what it was, or how much of an effort it took to craft? It was said that the first Tureg who had fashioned a necklace of the pearls was the first Regent of their fey. After gifting it to his pair, he ruled for millennia in happiness. The necklace was considered a good omen of substance and longevity.

From what Bret remembered that his father had told him, small globes formed on the underside of ledge rocks lodged deeply down the sides of tidewater flats in only one part of the garden. Each globe began as a pinpoint, breeding from the algae and fungal matter into oxygen. The growing pinpoint was encapsulated so that it was stable. Then it would swell in size and density until it was the size of a pearl, and malleable so it could be strung as a necklace. After a certain size, if the globes were not plucked, the encapsulation would dissolve, and the oxygen could escape into the atmosphere where it was originally intended.

There was only one chance to grab them. And that was right before a globe detached itself and floated up through the water toward the air. Right before detachment the globe sparked, signaling a leaving, and that was the instant it had to be taken. This oxygen making had gone on since the beginning of the firmament. Pure oxygen was a gift from the original creative spirit. These globes were now created sparsely, and never in great numbers, now that the garden had matured. He was determined to make one for Jondett, too, larger, more stunning, later, once all this business of the Celebration was over.

Well, so what if it was hard? As far as he was concerned, it should do the trick for Andrielle. A necklace like this was much better than a common necklace of round sand dollars and coquille shells. How hard could it be to catch a few bubbles anyway? He would try, and failing that, it was sand dollars and shells, there were plenty of those around.

Bret set out right away to the tidewater flats and hoped the seamless universe would help him out. Apparently it was the right time because he saw the telltale signs of bubbles popping and perking near half submerged boulders. The ocean beyond was curling up into generous waves, so he rode one down into the depths beside the ledge rocks. On the undersides were many globes generated by the lichen. What luck! He didn't know so many could form at once, the seamless universe was answering in abundance. He plucked as many as he could, and when he figured he had enough for a generous length, he flew back to the sweet grass field. There he found gossamer webs spider weavers spun each day. When the filaments were cut and dried, they became as strong as spun steel, light as a cloud. He sat there and created his necklace for Andrielle. The globes were white, and glowed with an intensity Bret had seen in fireflies. Surely Andrielle couldn't help but like this. Maybe he should tell a few of his friends where he'd found so many. They could go and gather some for a necklace, too. There were many more that he left. Maybe he'd have time to go back and make one for Jondett.

Colandid shook his robes as he sat down on his central quartz crystal in the middle of the Dantorak cavern. Jalenkad and Koyandel sat near Colandid. They waited for Colandid to speak with growing impatience.

"Aren't we going to do something?" Jalenkad was nearly beside himself. "We can't let them go through with this. It's just too much.

Things were so much better when they were at each other's throats. Aren't we going to do something?"

"Just try to simmer down. I'm willing to let them have a go at reconciling their differences. You know, when they're all together in one place it's much easier to send earthquakes or tornadoes their way, rather than two places. Just try to simmer down." Colandid turned a wry eye at Jalenkad.

Koyandel had something to say, too. "Colandid, if they patch things up, we will be outnumbered. That just can't happen. They'll unite against us. They'll try and stop us. Colandid, if they patch things up, we will be outnumbered."

"They'll be at each others' throats again. There'll be pressure on their resources, don't forget, and too much harmony is hard to take, even for the best of friends. They'll be at each others' throats again."

"Don't you realize how happy they'll be?" Jalenkad pointed out. "For a long time there will be harmony, one doesn't know how long it would take to make the resources diminish enough to cause problems. Don't you realize how happy they'll be?"

"It's all in how we do it. We could force resources to diminish, we could help the imbalances increase, and there are all kinds of problems we could create for them. We could even make trouble for their precious humans in more ways than they can fix. It's all in how we do it."

Jalenkad started muttering, "We should really collapse all the humans into our fey. They're the ones causing the problems in the garden. And maybe even try to find a way to bring the Tureg and Candela into the Dantorak. We'd all be one fey family. Call us the Dan-Tur-Dela, has a nice ring to it. But first things, first: we should collapse all the humans into our fey."

"It's always something to consider. Yes, it's always something to consider."

Colandid then stood up, signaling the end of their meeting, and pronounced the judgment. "Watch them carefully. Be observant and see how the Tureg and the Candela reconcile at the end of their so-called Celebration. It may work to their undoing after all. Watch them carefully."

Bret was ready to string the pearls when Zac came up to him. He was sitting in a quiet spot outside of the sweet grass field, away from the hustle and bustle of the preparations going on for the evening's feast. Bret thought he was out of view of his friends. He wanted to do this by himself.

"Bret, where did you find them?"

"I knew where to look."

"Listen, when the time comes for me to make my move on Kate, can you help me find some of them? I really want to give her something special. You know, Jondett is going to love that. Is that actually spider steel webbing, it's so thin."

"Zac, shut up. No, this is not for Jondett and you better not blab this around, ok? It'll just make her worried. No, this is for someone else."

"Who?"

"I can't tell you that."

"Come on, I can keep a secret – but I thought Jondett and you..."

"No, it's for someone else."

"Come on, Bret, what's the matter with you?"

Bret rolled his eyes up at his friend's insistence. What a nosey jerk. "It's for that Candela, if you must know, the one I had to go to Detention for."

"You must be joking. She's not worth it."

"She happens to be my teammate in this competition, I mean Celebration."

"Yeah, that's a tough one. No wonder you're going out of your way to make peace with her. She really has nice wings."

"Yes, she does, and her family is ok, too, the ones I've met. For Candela, I mean. Her brother Daniel teamed up with my sister Margaret, can you believe that? The way our two councils picked us as teams is crazy."

"You can't mean...you like her? She's Candela, Bret, you can't get involved with her, not if you're going to pair with Jondett."

"I know. Besides, they don't feel things like we do. They don't know numbers, either. No, I don't like the Candela like that. How could I? What in the garden makes you say that?"

"Oh, I don't know. You go out of your way to harvest the most difficult pearls in the garden. You worry about the pain you caused the Candela – it's just a bit unusual, that's all. As if you were really interested in her, at some level, anyway, that's all."

"Well, forget that. I just want this Celebration to turn out well, and I have to make peace with someone to whom I caused so much damage, I went to Detention."

"I know, I was there, too, don't forget. Um, Bret, I was thinking. If you're going to be so occupied with this Candela and all, would it be all right with you if I go and talk with Jondett now and then? Just to keep her busy, would you mind terribly?"

"Go do what you want, idiot. Just don't mention these pearls to anyone. Got it?"

"Sure thing, friend." Zac looked too happy flying off, Bret thought. What in the garden did he mean that the Candela was keeping him occupied? They were way too different. He'd have to find a good time to give the pearls to her. He thought about it. At the feast tonight? Too many fey around, he decided, especially his nosey jerk friends. Tomorrow before the competition ... that'd be perfect.

Preparations for the feast were well underway. Not that either of the fey could sense the other's unique gifts, but they sure tried to outdo each other. The Candela were intoning arias and trills worthy of the movement of stars, just to show the Tureg they knew what the garden was all about. The Tureg flashed numbers and equations up and down ladders of sequential obstructions, the streams of numerals swirling through both Candela and Tureg color spectrums. Music and numbers were incomprehensible to the other fey, but flares of colors from the warm and the cool spectrums were something that both fey could enjoy: yellow morphing into violet, green morphing into brilliant orange. Constant spectrum wheels of numbers and music blew about the sweet grass field, especially around the basalt and quartz crystal boulder. As far as touches and tastes, each Tureg and Candela felt and tasted on their own a myriad of the sundry and conflicting. What a seamless universe of senses!

Talandat and Magistrel called a halt to the preparations, everything was more than ready and it was time for the feast. Each raised their cup. Talandat's was made of gold entwined with platinum, and Magistrel's of platinum interspersed with gold. The juniper tonic was flowing, the braised sweet grass end stalks smelled delicious, the dogwood and juniper berry tarts stood ready for dessert. All Candela and Tureg had their fill and proceeded to the somnolent dance that ended the feast. Color and numbers whirled and pulsated to music created by the fey instruments. No Tureg or Candela had ever encountered such a mixed media, except for those that went back to the beginning of the firmament. Talandat and Magistrel toasted one another.

"This is a good beginning, Talandat, I must say."

"Magistrel, you are so right."

Both Regents had high hopes.

~ Chapter 16 ~

Bret woke earlier than he needed to the next day. Sleep had eluded him most of the night anyway. He flew to the fields hoping that Andrielle, too, was early. There she was, flying languorously around the boulder. She looked preoccupied. Bret set his shoulders, perked up his wings, and approached her. He was a study in discipline and control. He knew he had a hard sell ahead of him, and he didn't know if it was going to work or not, but here they were. He held out a flat box made out of leather to Andrielle.

"And just what is that?" Andrielle looked as angry as he'd ever seen anyone, his fey or theirs.

"Well, Andrielle – and by the way, my name is Bret—you might consider using it."

"I don't remember us being friends."

"If you'd consider this gift from one fey to another as an indication that I regret wholeheartedly our former confrontation, I would be most appreciative." Maybe this formal approach would work, he thought.

"You mean it's for my Regent?" She wasn't going to make this easy for him.

"Not at all, um, that is ..." He was at a loss for a minute. Then he stood up taller and had a serious set to his features. "This contains a gift for you, Andrielle, which I present to you in an effort to say I am sorry, and to overcome the sorrow I feel when I think of the hurt I caused you. I hope it will please you, and that the yellow sunbeams streaming out of you will continue until the end of time." This last bit was a totally unexpected, yet inspired thought. Bret surprised himself in speaking it out loud.

Andrielle took the box, opened the lid, and gazed down. A gasp escaped from her lips.

"I've only heard about these globes, I've never seen them." Her eyes took on a delight that only a swirl of cyclamen pink and alabaster opal could inspire, tympani thrumming and violas strumming in the background. Bret tasted peppermint and chocolate – what? Again with tasting something he wasn't eating? And what were the sounds bouncing around him? He could only watch as Andrielle took the string of pearls from the box, lifted it up and placed it around her neck. The pearls reflected her wings perfectly: aurora borealis to aurora borealis. Bret watched her smile, stroke the necklace, look up at him with the fierce sunflower beam and fly off. He was stunned, and very happy.

Andrielle could not believe it, a string of oxygen globes for her very own? Her sisters would be impressed, probably jealous. She wanted to tell Magistrel, and her mother and father as soon as possible. She approached her portal, touched the underside gill of the chanterelle, and dropped into the Candela cavern.

Grandel accepted her password and she flew up to her family's compartment. The sweet grass partitions were looking a little worse for wear after the earthquake, but that would soon change after harvest.

That morning Andrielle had awakened early, thinking too much, she realized. Chewing on the fact that she had to be teamed with that Tureg. She had flown to the boulder in the hopes of once again asking someone in charge to be released from this heinous team-up. And then this!

It was still early and few Candela had yet awakened to begin the day, but there was her mother seated at their table, knitting tiny hummingbird feathers into milkweed silk.

"What's got you so excited, Andrielle?" Gwen focused on her knitting and hadn't looked up yet.

"Mother, look at what that Tureg gave me!" She pirouetted around the table. She placed the box on the table. The leather box was encrusted with coquille shells and glints of shiny quartz. It was a work of art unto itself. But when her mother looked up and saw the necklace, she gasped.

"Unbelievable. I thought they were a thing of the past. Are they real, do you think?"

"Maybe they're not, in fact I hope not ... that'd be the end of him. I'm going to go and see if Magistrel can talk to me."

"Good idea, I'll go with you. For now put that back in the box." Gwen put aside her knitting and flew off with Andrielle to the knobbed table in the center of the Gathering space.

Magistrel looked up from the documents he'd been reading. He quickly pulled them together and put a blank sheet of foolscap onto the pile. "Ladies, nice to see you. What do you have there?"

Gwen took the box from her daughter and set it on the table. "Magistrel, that Tureg who'd abused Andrielle ..." before Gwen could finish, Magistrel turned to Andrielle, "Sorry, Gwen, let me ask Andrielle how she's doing."

"I'm all fine, Magistrel. Look at what Bret gave me."

"Bret?" both Gwen and Magistrel asked at the same time.

"Well, that's the name he gave me. All the Tureg are, well, you know, the enemy, but he did seem sorry."

"Tell us what happened," Magistrel leaned forward with a kindly expression. Gwen and Andrielle sat down.

"I woke early and went over to the boulder to do some thinking about all of this. Sorry, Magistrel, I was hoping there'd be someone there who would assign me to another Tureg. But there he was. He said he wanted to give me this for the hurt he caused me. Wait, that's not it. He said it's to overcome the sorrow he feels when he thinks of the hurt he caused me. I think that's right."

Magistrel took the leather box, and opened it. There glowing impressively was the necklace of oxygen globes. He sat back.

"Do you know what this is, Andrielle?" Magistrel asked.

"Is it real?"

"Yes, it is." Magistrel looked up at the ceiling. "Do you know what this is?"

"I know what it is. I've heard about them. It's a string of oxygen globe pearls. I've never seen anything in the garden as beautiful as they are." Andrielle smiled and sighed.

"More than that, obtaining these globes is a matter of chance, opportunity and vast serendipity. Globes of pure oxygen like this don't just happen. The right amount of algae, and fungal symbiosis has to occur. Then, water has to be clear and calm where the boulders sit in the tidal flats. Any little thing can cause the globes to be disrupted, or discolor, causing the oxygen to rise up to the surface to replenish the garden's atmosphere. When the globe itself detaches, the membrane covering it dissipates naturally, but when all things are right, then a flash occurs before it detaches. If someone is there at the right time, the globe can be plucked, and the membrane does not dissolve. It becomes what you see here: a beautiful string of pearls of the most valuable substance known in the garden. To have been able to collect these many and of such purity, your friend Bret had the seamless universe decide to help him. There is no other way that such a feat can be accomplished."

Gwen looked at Magistrel with curiosity. "Do you mean that there is a deeper meaning here?"

"Only the garden and the seamless universe know if something unusual was started when the Tureg gave this present to our Andrielle. Time will tell. Meantime, wear this string of pearls all the time – it is a sign of friendship. Perhaps a sign of something even more enduring."

"I can't stand the sight of him, Magistrel, but he did say something unusual at the end, come to think of it. He said he hoped the yellow sunbeams streaming out of me would continue until the end of time. Can you see any sunbeams coming out of me?"

Magistrel laughed. "He probably did not mean that literally, Andrielle. I think he was trying to tell you that he was sorry about the fall you took, what part he played in it, and that all things could be smoothed over. Why don't you ask him?"

Andrielle did not look happy at the prospect of having to talk to Bret about anything. But since Magistrel asked her, she would do it. Besides, her love of the beauty of the necklace was simply winning her over.

All fey teams were waiting for the nod from their Regents, to spur them to their tasks. Bret and Andrielle eyed each other, suspiciously on Andrielle's part, and anxiously on Bret's.

They'd been assigned to capture a falling star. A meteor, in other words. A meteor that would provide the garden with a spectacular perpetual light. That was definitely going to be a difficult task, but weren't all things worthy in the garden somewhat difficult? This Celebration was designed so that from the tasks many new things would come into being, to the benefit of the seamless universe. Who knew what would happen? Perhaps a team would come across a new species of plant or animal, or something even more rare, a new octave in the spectrum of music, or additional prime numbers. One team was assigned gathering whale song, another cloud bursts. Something Tureg might not even dream or care about. Or, it might be something that the Candela would not even care about or dream about. But what could they share? They were so opposite, what could they share?

As Bret and Andrielle walked away to the buffet table spread with breakfast offerings, he decided it was time to clear up a few things. He didn't want to criticize her. He wanted his questions to sound natural. He picked up a small cup of cucumber juice and an elderberry fritter.

"It's said that you Candela revere color and music and you can taste something based on what you are experiencing. Is that true?"

Andrielle fingered her pearls and cast him a withering glance. "Yes, our fey view music as part and parcel of life itself. What about you Tureg?" She was setting down her plate of rose petal cookies.

"Well, we spiral numbers at will, and the feelings we have from being with a friend or from the thought of something good produces happy backslaps, friendly punches to the chest. Warm lamb's wool on my face when I think of those I love."

"I taste something extraordinarily delicious when I think of my family or friends. Like vanilla crème, or a lovely peppermint on the tongue. It's a pleasure." Andrielle bent her head to one side, a small smile on her lips.

"Yes, a pleasure. But when I think of confrontation, or problems, I feel punches, scabs on my skin, not what I'd call pleasure. Like when we had that recent earthquake, or when I heard about the symbiosis we have with the Candela. The earthquake was real enough, and the punches and slams were real enough, too."

"I know what you mean, Bret. When that earthquake hit, it must have hit both of our fey at the same time. My fey, one after the other of my friends, said that they tasted the most horrid things: sardines soaked in bittersweet and vinegar was typical. Our spectrum colors were saturated with discordant hues, and the music, if you can call it that, was violent."

"It sounds like our numbers cause different color, and our senses cause different physical sensations to occur spontaneously. And, your music can cause different color, different tastes in the mouth. Maybe what we have between us is color."

"Maybe our team will find a new color. That could be what we contribute to the garden and the seamless universe."

Bret and Andrielle surprised themselves by looking into each other's eyes. There they found not only spectrums of colors, but music, numbers, the swelling of tastes on their tongues, and the soft lamb's wool floating over their shoulders. Andrielle found herself noticing Bret's light hair, the heft of his chin and his dark eyebrows over his serious eyes. His eyes that could cause her to fall into a serene dream... Just a minute, that's nonsense!

Bret was gazing into the bluest happiest eyes he'd ever encountered, her light hair floating around her face and down her shoulders over the light green robe she wore...if only he could keep looking at her forev... Wait, that can't be true!

Maybe they had something unforeseen in common after all.

They tore themselves away from each other gaze. It was time for their task.

One by one the Candela-Tureg teams flew off in all directions. Andrielle and Bret flew to the edge of the garden itself and they stopped to talk strategy, each one intent on not looking into each other's eyes. For this task, they knew that meteors were falling all the time from the seamless universe down through the firmament to their garden.

"We should have a plan," Bret said.

"Hey, you just stepped on my wing – what is wrong with you?"

"Oh, sorry, that is one of my faults ... my friends are always telling me that."

"Sure, along with the rest of your faults."

"Ok, ok, let's just forget that for a minute, can we? Getting back to the plan...."

Andrielle took a deep breath, and said, "Fine, but just watch what you are doing, will you? So, can't we just fly around up in the atmosphere and wait for a meteor to come to us?" She shrugged, shaking her wings a little. Several antrei fell off, much to her surprise. "Hey, now look what you've done."

"They looked like they were ready to fall off, anyway."

"Well, maybe. I'm going to put them in the baskets. It'll take me just a moment."

"I'm going, too, Andrielle." Bret wouldn't take no for an answer. "Our Regents would like that, don't you think?"

"Oh, I suppose you're right," she conceded. Bret gathered up the three scattered antrei and with Andrielle in tow, they flew back to the basalt boulder where antrei baskets were stowed, and where Talandat and Magistrel sat conversing.

"What have we here? Ah, antrei, good, very good. Magistrel, what do you think?"

"Yes, why not?"

Talandat turned to face Bret and Andrielle, each a strong young example of what was best about their two fey. "Bret and Andrielle, we've been talking about taking tours of each other's caverns. It's been such a long time, we decided that we would do that during the Celebration. Perhaps you'd like to take the antrei yourselves and place them in the nursery?"

There was no way that Andrielle's eyes could have popped open any larger.

Bret smiled at Talandat and nodded. "Leave it to me, sir."

Off they flew to the indigo bush by the sea, Bret leading the way followed by a very reluctant Andrielle.

Andrielle could not believe what she saw and heard when she and Bret sank down under the blue indigo plant. Not very different from the underside gill of the chanterelle that marked her home under the Vanderwolf pine. The portal keeper asked for a password and while odd sounding what with a number in it and something hitting granite, it vaguely reminded her of her own password, short and fluid.

It occurred to Andrielle that she was far from familiar surroundings. What in the garden is happening here? They have hurt and killed Candela. What kinds of torture traps are hidden here that Magistrel knows nothing about? Maybe she'd find herself captured and kept in a cell from which she could never escape, to live out her long life growing antreus after antreus for harvesting. Never to see another Candela in her life. Stunned and shocked by the thought, she could hear her own Regent sternly telling her to not be ridiculous, he would not have sent her into danger. So many secrets revealed, how many more were there? She shook off the dismal thought.

She followed Bret into the gathering space where there was a large knobbed chair, numbers swirling about it. She looked up toward compartments where she imagined Tureg lived. Could they be happy? How did they fly if they did not hear music? She did see faint numbers arranged in what she only could guess were configurations that meant something to someone. She glanced at Bret, who was intently studying her.

"What do you see here, Andrielle?"

"Well, there are faint images of numbers floating about in the swirls of color. They seem to be arranged in some kind of order, but that's not anything like I've ever seen before."

"Each family has equations of numbers that have grown out of our family bonds. So we are known by our combinations, and our compartments are identified that way, too. How are your compartments organized?"

"You actually do have families?"

"Of course, what did you think? You met my sister Margaret. So, what about your cavern?"

These Tureg were a surprise a minute. Andrielle shrugged, and answered, "Our compartments are arranged by musical keys, and our families intone music at the start of each meal." Andrielle stared at the numbers floating around. Some of them seemed to hover around Bret, who tilted his head to the left.

"Come on, let's go into the nursery."

Andrielle let Bret lead her into a side cavern and was stunned by what was before her. A large airy warm room with row upon row of baskets from which swirled colors in various stages of intensity and hue. Most of the colorations were a mix of warm and cool tones, shades of blue and green mixed with red and yellow. Some strong and some muted in intensity. Andrielle felt an instant affinity with what she saw.

"Why are some colors faint and others so bright? And what's making the colors?"

"I can answer that for you." A lilting voice behind her startled Andrielle since she thought she and Bret were the only ones there. One look at the Tureg who'd spoken told her she had nothing to fear. The lovely faced Tureg had long flowing dark wavy hair that reached nearly to her waist, and the sweetest smile and gaze imaginable. Her wings rose high above her head and draped down to knee length. She wore robes of some blue diaphanous material dropping below her knees. She was openly staring at Andrielle's wings.

"I am sorry to be rude and stare at you, but I have never seen a Candela before, and your wings are awesome. Where are my manners? My name is Jondett. Bret, why don't you introduce us properly?"

"Andrielle, I'd like to present Jondett of the Tureg fey. She is the head nurse of the Tureg ephemeral nursery."

Andrielle gasped and looked around the cavern "You can't mean that ... I mean ... this is where we all come from?"

Bret and Jondett's laughter sounded like silver bells. Jondett answered, "It's more complicated than that, but essentially, yes, every one of our Tureg and your Candela changelings begin as ephemerals. Infant loss is a plague on the dear humans. But we can transform an infant's ephemeral hope of life here in our cavern with the minor help of prairie smoke tendrils, and largely by Candela antrei. Are those antrei I see you carrying? They appear very healthy and just harvested. Oh, sorry, I mean gathered." Jondett looked gravely perturbed that she'd used a term that the Candela might find offensive.

Andrielle was too stunned by the tendrils of color swirls to be anything other than awestruck herself.

"Would you tell me how it happens?" she asked.

Bret began. "It's no secret. We Tureg rescuers are assigned the mission to go out to patrol hospitals and other places where human births occur. We rescue promising ephemerals from human babies once it's clear that their souls have returned to the original creative spirit. We transport the ephemerals back here to Jondett and her nursery attendants who place the ephemeral into a milkweed pod and surround it with prairie smoke tendrils."

Andrielle interrupted, "One of my friends is assigned the plant-insect ration and oversees wildflowers. Prairie smoke plants in particular on the flat plains of our garden's open land mass. I always wondered why that wildflower was singled out."

Jondett continued the explanation. "After a time, the ephemeral will require an antreus from the Candela wrapped around its emerging body to complete the transformation. Some of our Tureg have the duty to fly into the garden and pick up antrei after they have fallen from Candela wings. Sadly, when we are getting low, antrei have been taken." Jondett looked totally crestfallen as Bret continued.

"However, no Candela is ever supposed to be hurt. Our fey have enormous respect for Candela and we have punishment for those Tureg that harm one."

Jondett smiled at Bret, "As a matter of fact, Bret here recently came back from a finding mission where no antrei were found or gathered, even though there were some on the Candela's wings that were ready to fall off, and he could have done so with no harm at all to the Candela. For failing, he was sent to Detention. We are so glad he's back with us."

Andrielle felt a little guilty about that, but not too much. After all how was she supposed to know? She could tell the gaze that Jondett gave Bret spoke more than mere friendship. There were some interesting color spirals floating between them, too. She surprised herself by feeling a bit territorial about Bret, and that look on Jondett's face piqued her. She started to wonder about Tureg pairing, was it like Candela at all?

"Here are three antrei and more in the making." Andrielle took them from Bret and held them out to the beautiful Tureg. She saw that Jondett tore her gaze away from Bret and held her arms out to Andrielle.

"I have three little ones waiting right over here. Bret, maybe you'll remember that this one was in formation right before your last mission for ephemerals, and these two here were brought in right after the twins you rescued." The three baskets were swirling rose and green. Andrielle and Bret watched as Jondett went to three baskets and in each one carefully laid and tucked one antreus after another around the ephemerals.

"There, they are now ready for the last step."

"How long does it take?" Andrielle glanced up and down the rows of glowing baskets.

Jondett put a finger to her cheek and answered. "That's hard to say. Each ephemeral transforms in its own time. It could take many time sequences or few, for each step. First the prairie smoke tendrils, and then the antreus. Sometimes it's a long time between the tendrils and the antreus, sometimes just placing tendrils suddenly initiates the need for an antreus. It just depends on the ephemeral itself. We can't explain it, the seamless universe is a mystery."

Bret asked, "Where are the twins I brought in?"

"Right over here." Jondett flew over to the baskets in the next row. The colors that swirled up from two of them were indeed spectacular: deep rose with blue-grey tinges that flashed green and yellow.

"Andrielle, come look at these twin ephemerals. I visit the parents from time to time to see how they are doing. These twins have parents who grieve for them. They wish to have children and I hope they do. The love in that family is extensive."

"This is so much to take in! Do the human parents have any inkling at all?"

"So far, no, and our fey have not revealed that there is another purpose their lost children can serve."

"It makes me wonder who I was before." Andrielle was a study in wonder.

"We all wonder that. Every so often we Tureg will be inspired to name a changeling after its pre-rescue name," Brett said.

Jondett said, "We've been thinking that those twins could have their original names. Our the council will decide."

"What happens after they transform from ephemeral to changeling?" Andrielle asked.

Jondett answered. "A nursery attendant is always on call, watching. One of us sees the change from rose and green to either totally cool hues or warm hues. That alerts us that the ephemeral has become a changeling. We Tureg can see if numbers swirl, and if so we know the changeling is a Tureg. Without numbers we know it's Candela and they are taken to the sweet grass field where your Candela find them. Our own changelings stay here and are given to a worthy paired Tureg couple."

Andrielle looked surprised. "Our Candela pair too, and then the worthy ones are given a changeling to raise as their child."

"That's the way it's always been, since the beginning of the firmament and our garden."

Andrielle took a good look at the twins Bret said he'd rescued before his Detention term. Could it be that she saw numbers travelling up and down the spiraling color, or was it possible that only she heard the trilling notes sweetly combining to form key changes, discordant for the moment? Apparently not, for Bret looked as attentive to the transforming ephemerals as she did. It was only a momentary sensation, but she could swear that she once again felt a silk scarf settle around her shoulders. As she looked at Bret, she wondered if he tasted something—his mouth was making funny motions. She made a promise to herself that she'd ask him about that, once they were in the upper atmosphere looking for falling stars.

Bret could not contain his surprise at the taste of –what was that in his mouth? Yes, it was juniper berry compote. He loved the taste of juniper berry compote, especially the way his mother made it. But, hey, he wasn't eating any right now. He looked over at Andrielle who was brushing something off her shoulders, only to see that there was nothing there. Once back up in the atmosphere he wanted to ask her about that, and hoped it wouldn't be an intrusion. Thank the seamless universe she was wearing the necklace he'd given her. Perhaps she wouldn't mind answering a few questions. Jondett might have noticed the necklace, but she didn't say anything, so maybe she didn't. He'd have to make time to gather enough globes for a necklace for Jondett, too. It was something he wanted to do for her before they were paired. And he didn't have much time.

They flew out of the Tureg cavern and back to the basalt boulder.

Magistrel and Talandat were seated as before and looked intently at each of their young fey.

Bret could tell they wanted to ask them something and shrewdly started talking first. "Talandat, I took Andrielle for a quick tour of the cavern and the nursery. She got to meet Jondett and see the baskets of ephemerals."

"I've never seen anything like it! Has this been going on all the time?" Andrielle's puzzlement played out as discordant notes, and odd color swirls.

Magistrel answered, "Yes. Now you know how important it is that the Tureg and the Candela repair the terrible misunderstandings between us, don't you?"

Bret felt uncomfortable and looked over at Andrielle who looked sheepishly at him.

Andrielle answered, "I guess you could say we've both come a ways. I have a few questions ..."

"Why not go and capture that falling star? Your questions will no doubt be answered at the end of the Celebration. Go on and have some fun catching one of those things." Bret thought Talandat was a little slippery there, but nevertheless tilted his head away from Andrielle as if to say, let's go.

~ Chapter 17 ~

The two of them came to the end of the sweet grass field again where they'd left off, and stopped.

"Are you thinking the same thing, that we have to talk?" Andrielle looked pointedly at Bret.

"You better believe it! So tell me, why did I taste my mother's juniper berry compote? I also heard something like the flute playing we Tureg do."

"Why did I feel a silk scarf falling over my shoulders back there? And why is it that in the cavern I could see the swirls of numbers, just like I can see them hovering around your shoulders right now?"

"This is too weird, we have to go back and ask Talandat and Magistrel, don't you think? Maybe it's because we've been in contact and are trying to reconcile our differences? It's just that it's only when I'm around you that this happens, Andrielle."

"I think we'd better go back after we've caught a falling star. You know, it's only when I'm around you that I see floating numbers. I don't like it, it's very distracting."

"How do you think I feel being bombarded by sunbeams and tastes in my mouth when I'm not chewing anything, and then there's this ringing in my ears. It's so noisy."

"I hear music all the time."

"How do you put up with it? Doesn't it drive you crazy? How do you think with all that noise going on?"

"Probably the same way you think with all those shoves and pushes and the stuff clunking you on your head!"

"Nothing clunks me on my head – only when I'm mad."

"Oh, maybe that's it, then. Being angry at you caused things to hit me, your fault!" Andrielle stopped, blinked, then said, "But that silk scarf. Why that? It was in the nursery. Maybe because I couldn't help but feel tenderness being so close to the ephemerals. That was wonderful!"

Bret asked, "Why is this happening? I wonder if other Tureg and Candela teams are experiencing anything like this."

"Let's go get our falling star, Bret, first things first." Bret couldn't help but be impressed by the sunbeams blazing out around Andrielle as she laughed and took off. He followed.

Capturing a falling star was trickier than it sounded. Just at the right time, when the meteor entered the atmosphere of the garden, just when the light from burning up sprang from the detritus and created a line of light across the sky, just before it disappeared, a meteorite could be caught and compressed by a grid of spun steel spider webbing. It was as soft as gossamer, but unbelievably strong. The gossamer was similar to what the oxygen globes were strung with. Within that grid, the explosion of light would compress smaller and smaller to become a steady glow, a perpetual beacon for all time. True fey lights that would make mica glow, be the reflection in obsidian, or light up any space the fey wanted lit. Not a bad thing to have in the garden, by any standard.

Bret and Andrielle were flying with a backpack filled with just the right amount of gossamer, in search of a meteor.

Colandid did not know exactly what was going on with the Tureg and the Candela but he could take a good guess. They were having a great time reconciling. They were making the garden better for the people. How ghastly. He fingered the cascade of minerals on a string by his side. Cabochons of garnet and turquoise shook as he stroked the string. Irregular amber beads like drops of sun quivered between the cabochons. He finally gave up and thought that time was going to tell if indeed this reconciliation was something that the seamless universe would tolerate, or if the seamless universe was telling him to react once again.

Besides, Colandid knew his spies would get in touch with him. Those two Tureg in Detention were just the type of fey that came along once in a millennium, and it wasn't long before Colandid had made contact with them in the watery depths. It was easy really to convince them to cause some havoc to that so-called Celebration. They wanted to, it was in their nature to despise Candela. And, they were not the two brightest stars in the sky. The duller the better. Gerhardt and Concret kept Colandid informed of what was going on, and he made them think it was for the good of the seamless universe. No good would come of Tureg and Candela making peace, what did they think they were doing?

Cancret and Gerhardt secreted themselves outside the sweet grass staging area looking on while team after team received their assignments and flew off. They were not some of the Tureg chosen to team up with Candela. Understandably, they hadn't proven themselves to Talandat that they really could be trusted that far. There was too much history of gratuitous violence during antrei gathering, so they were made part of the watches that patrolled the garden, monitoring the small cracks in the earth, which made it very easy to drop messages down to the Dantorak.

"Look, we have to do something and soon. This 'Celebration' is a farce, why is it that only you and I know it?" Gerhardt shifted his bulk behind a large clump of bloodroot while Cancret peered over fern fronds.

"What I wouldn't give to grab some of those Candela and show them what for." Cancret turned to his friend. "You know, we've harvested so many antrei for the nursery our knuckles bleed. It's not fair that we're supposed to cozy up to the those fly-faces."

"We have to have a plan. I want to keep at least two or three of those teams from delivering. There must be something we can do."

"Those squirrely Dantorak fey we met at the edge of Detention were something. They'd do the right thing by us, if we could wreck something."

"If we followed one of the teams, we'd find a way. What about it?"

"Good. Let's follow the next one out. Hey, it's Bret. I've wanted to get back at him. He's teamed up with the Candela he went to Detention for. Can you believe that? What a punch in the gut to the seamless universe."

"If we keep watch on them, something will happen so that we can, you know, make it unhappen. If you get my drift."

"Yeah. They're taking off. They're supposed to collect a falling star, isn't that revolting?"

"Puke. Let's take up some rose thorns with us. That'll make quick work of their spider webbing. I don't care how hard their webbing is, rose thorns will take it out."

"Yeah. Well, this'll be one meteor won't light up any garden any time soon!"

It was as serene as both Bret and Andrielle were told that the upper atmosphere could be. Below were clouds swirling, changing colors and shifting from place to place while dissolving and blending into huge thunderheads, and then breaking apart into streaks of clouds briefly illuminated by the sun. The clouds reminded them of waves upon waves, churning and glistening, and strangely like a floor they could walk on. Very similar to the wakes of boats and ships, shifting, dissembling, riddled and combed.

They saw rainbows appear and disappear time and again as they stood their watch. At one time it was Tureg mission to patrol this upper atmosphere for meteors and divert them. Some large ones had eluded the Tureg and wreaked havoc on the garden, but it was generally conceded the seamless universe had permitted things to happen like that. Now that he knew about the Dantorak, Bret surmised that the seamless universe had nothing to do with any of the collisions.

The garden had its share of large meteors in the past, and it was now only small ones that actually burned up in the upper atmosphere causing light shows that the people and fey enjoyed seeing. At least the meteors looked small from the surface of the garden.

"Bret, did you see that rainbow? I guess you see colors, right?" Andrielle's tone was a lesson in restrained sarcasm.

"Yes! That one there just gave me a bear hug. You know I perceive colors. And I feel them, too. Plus there are always numbers bouncing around me. Here they look simply free and happy as if they were playing hopscotch."

"I heard trumpets and flutes, oboes in the background. I tasted, I think, some kind of sassafras tea, bubbly and delicious."

The two of them were conscious of their innate differences, but then Andrielle admitted, "Of course, now and then I shiver when I see numbers floating in some of the clouds. That's very weird for me. I hope I get used to it, if that's the way it's going to be from now on."

"I can taste a slight peppermint flavor in my mouth. The humming isn't so bad anymore, just weird."

"When did it start for you?"

"Since I saw you under the Rosa rugosa."

"The seamless universe is playing tricks on us, Bret. Magistrel says I'm the only Candela he's heard of who senses numbers and he's been waiting a long time for that to happen."

"When did it start for you?"

"The first was when we collided, and then I also felt something land on my shoulders, something like a soft blanket, you know?"

"Sure, I feel that a lot when I'm with friends or family."

"Ah, friends, too, besides a family."

"Don't start in on that again. Don't you have a family, and friends?"

"Well, yes, all Candela live with their families until they are paired. I have tons of friends. You're going to have a tour of our cavern. You'll see."

"Um, we live with our families until we are paired. Does your pairings happen at the end of harvest, like ours?"

"When else, I mean, sure they do." Bret saw that Andrielle had been looking at him now and then during this conversation, albeit with skepticism. He saw the necklace he gave her glowing on her neck.

"Hey, look, I think I see a meteor coming this way!" Bret was astounded at the size of the rough edged boulder tumbling down to the garden's atmosphere. He and Andrielle started to unfurl the spun steel gossamer net when streaks of color flashed in front of them, and their net fell apart in their hands.

"Andrielle, are you all right?" Bret saw Andrielle's eyes flash fright. A hurricane strength wind caused by the streaks tore the net apart and blew most of it away. All that was left was shards. Bret tasted bitter orange and unsweetened sorrel.

"Oh my garden, what was that? No, I'm fine, Bret. But wow, I really got punched in the stomach."

"Look at the webbing. There's hardly any left, it's no good anymore. What caused that?"

"I think this is our culprit." Andrielle showed Bret the rose thorn embedded in the handful of webbing she had left.

"By the seamless universe, now we have to go back and gather spider webbing to make spun steel again. This will really put us behind."

"Never mind that, we could have been killed!"

"Hey, you're right! Who did this?"

"Everyone I know wants this Celebration to work between our two fey. Doesn't your fey?"

"As far as I know. When I was in Detention – hey, wait a minute, there are two guys I know, well, I don't really know them. They're kind of outsiders. They like nothing better than to beat up Candela when they can. We all knew about them, but they were sneaky. Finally they were caught and put in Detention at the same time I was. I don't think those two ever really got it, if you know what I mean."

"Do you think they're responsible for this?"

"There's only one way to find out. We have to set a trap."

"I think I know what to do." Bret listened to Andrielle lay out the plan, his admiration for her growing by the minute. "Pyrethrum gel prevents roses from growing the points on their thorns, so it should be a good shield for our net. I have some because we're given it to help out in our patrols in the gardens."

"I can't believe steel-strong spider webbing was so easily destroyed."

"Yeah, but we can catch them!"

"Let's do it!"

Back in the fields, both Andrielle and Bret began the arduous task of gathering spider silk from which the spun steel netting could be weaved. They kept their eyes open for Cancret and Gerhardt. Sure enough there they were, Bret saw, lying comfortably sunning themselves, wings open, on flat boulders. He motioned to Andrielle to come with him to the central basalt boulder where Talandat and Magistrel were overseeing everything, checking off teams as they brought in their tasks, and generally holding court. There was a great deal of festivity around the boulder, including those who were setting up for the banquet.

"Talandat and Magistrel, we come before you with a sore point. Both Andrielle and I had a meteor in our grasp when all of a sudden flashes of color ripped our netting to shreds and caused us to lose our falling star. We're beginning to gather enough spider silk to begin again, but we wanted to tell y ..."

Magistrel looked doubtful, "My dear fey, do you think someone sabotaged your task and wished to harm you?"

"Well, we think it was suspicious ..." Bret began.

Magistrel continued, "Who or what could have done this to you? Perhaps there were several falling stars about you, and that caused the ripping?"

Talandat weighed in, "Let's consider this a near miss, shall we? Before we try to blame someone for disrupting the Celebration. Of course, if you'd like to press the point, it would be better done when you actually have captured a fallen star." Talandat's expression gave them an indication of how much he believed them.

Both Andrielle and Bret looked at each other. "Well," began Andrielle, "maybe that was it. Come on, Bret."

Bret and Andrielle turned away and went back to the fields to collect their spider silk.

"Why didn't you mention the rose thorn?" Andrielle asked Bret as she flew into the sweet grass and gathered a large web.

"They weren't going to buy it, I could tell. They would have said that the thorn was in there to begin with. Anyway, I'll tell them after we catch those two. It'll be proof positive, you know?"

Carefully they took the spider silk from the web and wound the strands around lemon verbena branches. The wood held the silk threads loosely and let them dry. With witch hazel wands quick-clicking, both Andrielle and Bret wove the dry threads into netting. Even though dry spider silk was as strong as steel, it was not impervious to rose thorns. Andrielle applied a generous layer of pyrethrum gel to every strand in the netting.

"I still believe it was the two guys I told you about. When we go up into the atmosphere, let's spread out the netting, and ride a meteor down into it, maybe we could catch both of them at the same time!"

"Good plan."

Andrielle and Bret started out for the upper atmosphere and were careful to watch who was following them this time.

"I just felt a kick to my ribs, Bret!"

"Me too, and I'm tasting the most putrid slop!"

"Yuck, it's the worst ever. It appears we have a bad tailwind!"

Both of them flung out the netting and sure enough Gerhardt and Cancret were caught in the trap, bound up like the thugs they were. Bret and Andrielle could see the two of them hacking at the netting with thorn studded branches, but it didn't work. They carted the large hunkering bundle back to the sweet grass field and plopped it down beside the boulder where Talandat and Magistrel were talking with some of their council and a few Tureg-Candela pairs were returning from their tasks.

"Caught these two following us," Bret looked very pleased with himself.

"We didn't do nothing! We were just minding our business, patrolling like we're supposed to, and suddenly they throw a net on us!" bellowed Gerhardt trying mightily to free himself.

Magistrel wagged his head from side to side as he said, "You mean you were patrolling cracks in the garden, way up in the atmosphere? The better to see them, what, long distance?"

Talandat looked stern. "How dare you ruin what we're doing here? You're not smart enough to come up with this idea. Who put you up to it? Who?"

By this time, Cancret and Gerhardt had extricated themselves from the netting and stood sullen and still. "Nobody put us up to nothing."

"And with that, you've just earned yourselves more Detention time." Talandat added, "You're confined to the cavern, until after harvest."

Looking stunned, the two were led off toward their portal by hefty Tureg security guards.

"Well, Bret and Andrielle, it looks like your netting is still in good shape. Why don't you two go up and see if you can find your falling star?" Magistrel shooed them both away.

Once they were out of hearing, Magistrel proposed, "If you're thinking what I'm thinking, we have to meet with the Dantorak and get a few things settled. Now they've gone and made spies out of two Tureg. This has to stop, it's not right." Talandat was pacing again. Magistrel sat down on the boulder, chin on his fist. "You know, more is at stake here. Bret and Andrielle were able to resolve enough conflict between them to come up with a way to catch the spies. They're working together better than I thought they would. We can't let the Dantorak ruin that."

Talandat stopped his pacing to say, "Let's drop a message down one of the cracks. They'll find it."

~ Chapter 18 ~

"Fine," Colandid said as he read the message. "I'll meet with them. It's been a long time. Maybe they need to realize how far they've gone with those wretched humans. Fine."

The message made its way back to the basalt boulder. A warm lava flow carried it up halfway, and then the iron ions magnetically transferred the message the rest of the way. It rose up out of a quartz fissure right beside the two Regents.

"Shall we invite him to one of our caverns? Or right here?"

Magistrel stroked his beard and answered, "It should be somewhere more neutral. How about at the edge of Detention? We'd all be safe with Cam and his crowd patrolling."

"Agreed. Let's send Colandid an answer to his message."

The Sargasso Sea gleamed alive and well lit at the edge of Detention. Cam hung motionless as he waited for his guests to arrive. Quarters had been prepared for the meeting. Just as he'd arranged long ago when the three fey met regularly.

Cam wondered what was up with them. Could it be that their attention was finally directed to the waters? The endless sea covered three fourths of the garden, and yet the fey had not troubled themselves very much with what was going on here, beyond the simple and superfluous. The destruction of coral reefs was only minimally attended to, and the patrolling of destruction and reconstitution of sand beaches was fine, but so many species were waiting to be catalogued and when were the fey going to do that? He knew about their mission of watery depths, yet wondered how many of them actually took that seriously. And, how he wished the fey cared more for the people who explored the depths. Humanity would benefit from that, and wasn't that one of the fey missions? More was going on under the surface of the seas than on land. The seamless universe had given the garden so much. More missions and maybe even more communities of fey were needed. Only the seamless universe knew.

Three figures made their way to the Detention entrance. The tall pale one rose up from one of the fissures in the sea floor, and two others were floating down to the depths. Colandid, Magistrel and Talandat took their seats in view of those that patrolled Detention. All three were from the first laugh, the first diaspora, the first existence of fey. All three of them along with their fey had agreed upon the separation pact. Their missions and innate differences set each of them apart, yet wisely all knew that what each of them represented would together be strong and complete. Back then, they knew their combined gifts would repair the destructive ruptures to the garden that the pressure of creation produced. If it wasn't a sinkhole, it was a flood. Or, creation threw rock so high new mountains were made. That caused trouble on so many levels. Water – land – air balances, destruction of flora, destitution of predators so that minor animals and rodents increased, always the insects. It continued to be a struggle to maintain the delicate balance.

Their pact to jointly care for the garden had for many millennia been weakened, and now was the time to strengthen it, for the good of the garden.

"Thank you, Colandid, for meeting with us." Talandat took the lead.

"I take it that the two of you have always been in contact, is that right? I've always suspected it, you know. I take it that the two of you have always been in contact, is that right?"

"Yes, we were above ground and even when our ignorant feud kept our fey apart, the two of us maintained contact." Talandat looked over at Magistrel. Both of them gave each other an amused look over the doubling up of the Dantorak speech pattern. One day that was going to trip them up.

"Yet you did not believe that I could have been of help? How can you not know that we Dantorak were and continue to be the most supportive fey of this garden? Yet you did not believe that I could have been of help?"

"Now you can, if you're willing. We are attempting to settle the feud between us. Will you help?"

"You know we have separate interests. Humans are destroying the garden. You know what they are. Uranium, one of the garden's gifts, is openly available as the seamless universe decreed. All the minerals are at the behest of the humans as the original creative spirit dictated the fruits of creation. Yet, all we do is clean up their mess. Don't you see they can't be trusted? You enable them to continue their destruction. You know we have separate interests."

Magistrel had kept quiet until now. "Colandid, we were brought forth from humans, and our very existence depends on them. You take a full grown human as a Dantorak. It's true that you could even take them all. The reason you do not is that the original creative spirit did not decree that you should."

Colandid threw his shoulders back. "Many of my council think it's time for drastic measures against the humans. But cool heads have always prevailed and I for one am against it. It's the humans that provide the Dantorak with fey, and you with your ephemerals. Our replenishment comes from only those who are truly lost, and without our help, they would not have a better purpose. People lost in the wilderness of nature, or their own minds, or born with such distractions that their lives are self-destructive. You know who they are. They can have a new purpose. Even the biggest bullies, the most heinous criminal or addict might offer something. So when they wander into lost regions, we assess if we can gather them into our way of life. To rebuild them. The seamless universe is mysterious. Our Dantorak are true survivors. Your ephemerals are also, but with a difference. They've never been tested in the real human world, and been reborn. Ours have. Many of my council think it's time for drastic measures against the humans."

"Yes, clearly that is so different, coming from knowing what does not contribute to the seamless universe into what does," Magistrel took the lead now. "And our ephemerals have not experienced destructive elements of life. They are innocent. This is food for thought for another time. I relish conversations, and the resolutions between us three that will come from our accords. But now we have a very immediate problem. How can we heal the feud that mars Tureg and Candela collaboration? Let this Celebration continue without harm, think about helping us settle things between us. Call off your spies, your discontented few in the Tureg, and maybe in the Candela for all I know, and then all three fey can tackle the big problems. Such as pollution, land mining, fish depletion, ecological disasters the people are responsible for. What are the Dantorak doing to protect and enhance, as is your directive, as I remember it?"

Colandid began, "Our mission is to protect the balance of the garden's mineral resources. We oversee lava formations that produce new land, and hydrothermal vents that produce new species. More than you know. When all is stable and in balance, then your fey can assess other consequences in the garden. That is your directive, is it not? Our mission is to protect the balance of the garden's mineral resources."

"We are in agreement as we've always been." Talandat had begun to pace.

Magistrel said, "The imbalances have been artificially enhanced because of what's been going on between Tureg and Candela. That can now be put to rights. And we believe it's going to happen, and we want it to happen. The Dantorak should, too." Magistrel sat down after pronouncing this.

"The humans are going to benefit. No doubt in a way that will cause more and more imbalances. The humans are going to benefit."

"Colandid, the seamless universe decreed that people exist. None of us can go against that directive and you know it." Talandat had stopped and stared at his old friend, his old adversary.

"I know it's true." Colandid fingered his crystals and they shone and reflected the light. "It just galls me to no end that humans make us suffer when we repair the problems they create. I tell you two..." Colandid stood up and pointed at Magistrel and Talandat. "Perhaps the seamless universe is depending on the Dantorak to set things right in the garden. Haven't you ever thought about what it would be like if only the three fey existed here? We'd have no human problems to repair, no imbalances to sort out. Yes, we came from the first human, but perhaps we are supposed to exist far longer. Think about it, Magistrel and Talandat, and when you do, maybe you'll see that you've been very lenient with those who have taken advantage of you. I know it's true."

Before Colandid turned away to go back to his home cavern, he gave both Magistrel and Talandat this warning. "I won't interfere any more in your so-called Celebration. But know this. A synchronicity between your two fey is immaterial to the larger problem of the humans themselves. I won't interfere any more in your so-called Celebration." And with that he sunk into the crevasse that appeared at his feet.

Magistrel and Talandat were astonished to hear what Colandid said before he disappeared. Talandat began to pace, and Magistrel looked off to the far distances as he sat back down. Chin in hand. It was clear both were seriously pondering Colandid's threat.

~ Chapter 19 ~

"We got one!!" Andrielle never looked so lovely as now. Bret cherished this moment as she pulled on the netting with both hands and approached his side to close it tight over their prize: a fallen star. As their hands closed around the top of the netting to totally enclose the star, they had flown very close to each other. Their faces were close, and the tips of their top wings touched, producing sparks, a light show, simple sums and keynote trills swirling in their colors, now compressed to its substantial essence. He pulled on his side and approached Andrielle. How could he not have foreseen that he was so enchanted by her? The sunbeams were the first clue, and now this.

"What in the garden..." Bret could tell that his worry was beside the point, as Andrielle smiled, and glittering beams surrounded them both. They lost all sense of time.

Later on, they brought the fallen star back to the basalt boulder in the middle of the sweet grass field. Both sat side by side, next to their bundle, a study of serious wonder.

"This must be a first, don't you think?"

"Andrielle, it's a first all right. What, really, happened?"

"I thought that our two fey did not mix, we are so different, and besides which, in my lifetime, Tureg are the enemy."

"In my lifetime, Candela are the enemy."

"I think I need some time away from numbers and fluffy clouds, if you know what I mean." Andrielle stood up and looked sweetly at Bret, with a smile. "I'll see you at awards dinner tonight." Bret watched her fly off, thinking, her wings were incredibly beautiful.

Bret sat still at the boulder watching other teams bring in their tasks. He saw his sister Margaret and Andrielle's brother Daniel. They were supposed to weave a fishnet that would ensnare a lie. Any fey who had one of these surely had an upper hand, especially if he wanted to avoid going to Detention. With one of them sensing numbers and the other music, this task should have been an easy one. But as he glanced at his sister, her look of disgust was apparent. Clearly things did not go as well as it did for Andrielle and him. He flew off following Margaret to the Tureg portal and then into their family compartment. Once there, Margaret burst into tears.

"How could they team me up with that Candela? It was horrible. I'd weave a color into the net, and he claimed he could see it. But then he'd throw in something I couldn't see, and it would rip a hole in the fabric! He couldn't taste anything, and he kept droning on and on about how my musical scales were too complex for the netting. It was so frustrating!"

"Did you taste anything?"

"What are you talking about?"

"Did you sense any numbers at all?"

"Oh please, for the garden's sake, Bret. It's hopeless."

"Margaret, come on, let's go back to the boulder and find Daniel. I'll go with you. You know, he's not a bad fey, you should have seen him work during the earthquake. Don't give up just yet, I have an idea."

"Better be a good one."

Back at the boulder off to one side was Daniel.

Bret said, "Why don't you two try to combine numbers and music, you might surprise yourselves." The two of them stared at Bret as if he were crazy, but in the end they flew off resigned to try once more, grumbly and grim.

Seeing they were well on their way, Bret turned to see that Zac was standing next to Jondett. She must have completed her shift in the nursery, and flew here to see what was going on. Zac must have finished the task he and Pamela were assigned. Bret was looking forward to seeing what new wildflower they'd discovered.

"Hey you two, what's going on?"

Jondett turned to him with a fire in her eyes he'd never seen. "You gave that Candela that necklace?!"

"Well, yes ... I was sent to Detention because of her."

"Maybe you need to go back there." And with that, Jondett spiraled a huge color flare and flew off, allowing no word of reply from Bret. He fell back in shock.

"What ... wha ..."

Zac led him off to the side. "Bret, my friend, did you really think that Jondett was not going to find out that you, the fey she committed to pair with, for all time, gave a priceless object that the seamless universe allows to be created only rarely, if that, to another fey—especially a Candela? Are you THAT dumb?"

Bret gave a puzzled look, and said, "Zac, I think I need some quick advice."

"Yes, pal, you sure do."

Once Zac got started, Bret couldn't shut him up. Bret couldn't help wondering, does he think I'm a moron?

"Look, I'm your friend so I'm going to explain a few things to you."

"Oh yeah, what things? Are they from that deep well of wisdom you think you have?"

"Go ahead, pal, be funny. Jondett is mad at you. Do you know why?"

"It looks like she wanted that necklace."

"Bravo! However, that's the smallest of your concerns."

"I love Jondett, I want to be paired with her ... for all time ..." Bret felt some misgivings as he said this. Why was that?

"It's not the necklace, you moron, it's what giving the necklace to someone means. Don't you get it?"

"I thought ... I'm ..." Bret rose up and anger surged into him. "Look, just keep your opinions to yourself. It's none of your business. This is between Jondett and me, so stop it, right now."

"Sure, I'm just telling you."

"And I'm warning you – butt out!"

Bret felt rotten blasting Zac, but now was the time for thinking, not talking. He flew back to his family compartment, and finally settled into his room, his own butterfly weed pod bed, and his own thoughts.

Andrielle flew fast and furious to her portal, dropped in, and found her mother where she knew she'd be, thank the seamless universe. Her father was nowhere to be seen, probably at the Celebration site, thank the seamless universe again.

"Mother, I'm in trouble, I think."

Gwen put down her witch hazel rods with which she'd been weaving a tapestry, and focused on Andrielle. "Sit down, sweetheart, I'm here for you."

With Andrielle looking forlorn, it all came out. How the numerals were more and more apparent, especially around the Tureg Bret. How simple brushes on her skin or touches she felt on her cheek could not be explained, especially around Bret. How these things happened with greater frequency, always around the Tureg Bret. Andrielle looked confused as she explained the latest of her worries.

"Mom, what does it mean when our wingtips touch and then sunbeams surround us? I felt so wonderful. As I looked up, I saw more and more of the stars exploding in the sky. It seemed as if there were only the two of us in the vast firmament. I wanted it to go on forever and forever. The thought of him, the music of him, surrounded me."

Gwen's mouth dropped open. Then she recovered, sighed and said, "That means, my dear child and grown-up daughter, that you and the Tureg are paired."

Andrielle did not think that her mother heard her right. "Look, Mom, you weren't there. It was a nice feeling and all, but come on, that wasn't—pairing?—was it?" Andrielle's brow furrowed. "What are you talking about?"

"This is all my fault. Remember what I told you about grown-ups, how they pair after the harvest? I haven't told you what exactly happens since you are, I thought, not ready to hear that. It's very beautiful and symbiotic, and what the seamless universe wants for us: communion with another until all of the cells in our bodies coincide and become one. This communion then becomes a psychic connection that reoccurs time and time again. It will not ever happen with another, and so pairing signifies the beginning of a fey's life with a mate. As a grown-up fey, pairing fulfills our needs beyond what as individuals we can. It's a gift given to us, complete harmony with another, peace and fulfillment beyond understanding. Looks like your mother did you a disservice, my dear Andrielle, for not explaining this to you earlier."

"Are you sure? It happened so fast. Our wingtips touched, so what? I don't remember what happened afterward, neither did Bret for that matter. What happened?"

"Yes, I'm very sure. You are paired. With paired Candela, like your father and me, the first connection is spontaneous with a great burst of energy. With each connection, more and more of the synchrony deepens. Fondest hopes become possible, our music harmonizes, our colors become variants of each other. We taste the same things. It makes us one. The first time is very special and because it is, the pairings always take place after harvest. During the grand Celebration, as part of the Candela rite of Continuation. The new-to-be-paired are given something one could call instructions, but in reality the words are inspirational, there's no instructions. To be ourselves, so as to be better able to contribute to the seamless universe. Then off the pairs go, seeking privacy for their first connection."

"We were up in the atmosphere, it was private all right. But if I'm paired with a Tureg – does this mean that it's for all time, or ..."

"I think it's time to go find Magistrel and ask him a few questions. This pairing is simply beyond what I know, my dear daughter, can't you see that?" Andrielle could see the tears starting, and the love expressed in her mother's eyes.

"I'm pretty sure Magistrel is at the boulder in the sweet grass fields."

"We better get going, so we can get this taken care of before awards night. Your father needs to know, and he's coming with. I suppose it's best that I tell him. Where is he?"

Bret uncurled from his fetal state where he'd lain for some time. His father had called his name. Selat was insistent that Bret join him at the family table.

As he stumbled into the room, Selat was looking at him with thunder in his eyes. He knows, thought Bret.

"Are you a moron? You gave a valuable object to a Candela?"

What was this moron thing?

"You're out of line here, father. That necklace was to help me say I'm sorry to Andrielle for hurting her and..."

Before Bret could continue, his father exploded, "What in the name of the seamless universe are you talking about! Think about what you are doing! Your whole future is at stake – you're supposed to be paired with Jondett, her family is expecting it, our family is expecting it. What's wrong with you?"

"Hey, it was the right thing to do, something to say I'm sorry – haven't you done the same thing time and again for mother?"

"That's different!"

"No, it isn't. And why do I sense this noise around her, noise that trills up and down the whole forsaken universe..."

"Don't swear – I mean it, Bret!"

Bret sank into a chair and looked forlorn. "It's so distracting. I don't know what I'm doing anymore. And then, without warning I taste things I'm not eating.... What's going on, Father?"

"Well, let's all calm down, now. Me, too." Selat began pacing around the table. "You say you are still hearing and tasting things. That is very odd for a Tureg, to say the least. What else, son?"

Bret looked at his father. This was the fey who'd brought him up, who'd given him the missions and purposes he maintained as a Tureg, who advised him and dealt with him squarely and fairly all his life. Who loved him. "Father, there's something else about the Candela I need your advice on."

Selat stopped pacing. He looked straight at Bret and said, "What else have you done?"

"Well, up in the atmosphere, we were catching a meteor and then when we were closing our net around it, our wingtips touched. Suddenly, way up the atmosphere, away from anyone, sunbeams surrounded us. I lost some memory of what next happened but I can tell you this—I will always protect Andrielle and provide for her well being all the time I have left."

"Yet, on the other hand, you're supposed to pair with Jondett."

"Yes, and I also know Jondett is angry with me for giving the necklace to Andrielle."

"Son, this may be a first for both of our fey, Tureg and Candela. Are you aware that from what you've told me, this means that you are now paired. And with a Candela. I can't believe a Candela is my daughter in law!" Selat sat down heavily, with a dumbfounded look on his face. His wings began a dirge-like waving, and his numerals began spinning prime numerals. This was traumatic. Bret hoped that his father's numerals would stop. They were deep and distracting, not to mention the taste of rotting grapefruit he tasted in his mouth. And what did his father's explanation mean, that he was paired with a Candela? Jondett and he had an understanding, and no wingtips were going to make any kind of a difference on that at all. He'd take care of the mix-up as soon as possible.

"Father, are you all right? This is just a misunderstanding, I can take care of it."

"Yes, I'll be all right, I guess. It's just the thought that you are now a paired fey, with a household to provide for, perhaps changelings to raise in time. What changelings? Where are they going to come from? Oh, the seamless universe, I have to tell your mother."

They both looked up when at that moment Sulpicett poked her head into the living area. "Hey, Bret, did you and that Candela get your falling star? I was watching for a while, and came home early to organize my offering for the feast. Everyone loves my juniper berry compote. I was thinking of making it, just in case there was so much Candela food that at least we'd have something to eat." She chuckled at her own joke, and pattered on while pulling juniper branches from their baskets and plucking the deeply hued berries.

She stopped and did a double take at Bret. "Wait a minute, why are you here?"

"Dear, wait until you hear what Bret has managed to do – he's now a paired fey. Can you guess with whom?"

"Sounds like Jondett and you just couldn't wait and found your own time. Naughty, naughty, Bret." His mom was smiling as she shook her finger at him.

As Selat relayed the news to Sulpicett, her expression went from light to dark, and Bret felt slaps on his face, his cheek pinched hard, unlike the gentle pinching he used to feel as a changeling. Another bruising slap, this time really hard. She was not taking this well.

"Come on, you're jumping to conclusions. Jondett and I have an understanding. I'll just explain things to her, and our Regent can work something out, can't he? To make things right?"

Both Selat and Sulpicett looked at each other and their son saw some kind of unspoken communication pass between the two of them. Just the kind of pairing he wanted with Jondett, easy connection with someone he loved. He thought so anyway, which was why he proposed pairing in the first place. And she accepted, hadn't she?

"Bret, this is far beyond anything I know about in our fey." Sulpicett had stopped picking juniper berries off branches long ago. "We'd better go to Talandat and seek his council. He goes back to the first sparks of laughter, so maybe he can tell us what to do."

Bret was shaken. They're serious. I'm in trouble. "I think we can find him at the boulder."

Both Magistrel and Talandat were still checking off the teams as they flew in and presented their fulfilled tasks. Madison and Trent showed both Regents the starfish they found. A new type from the edge of the garden where colorful starfish live and breed. This was a new strain, and it would bring forth new colors in the garden, especially in wildflowers, the better to protect them from insect and disease. Mitchell and Kate were lugging the largest basalt boulder they'd ever seen, but this one was unique. Fey could ionize the air by pulling it through the garden. This would clear out particulates, making the air clearer and clearer. It would be invaluable when humans burned off smelly coal. Also during wildfires. One by one the bundles filled the area around the boulder, and many hands were needed to get things organized before awards night. Even the fishnet that Margaret and Daniel managed to construct was finished. It was clear that both were thrilled as they told their story to whomever they could collar.

Both Regents were impressed with the results.

Talandat couldn't help but remark, "This is incredible, Magistrel. I haven't seen so many wondrous objects in a long time."

"I really like the way those sticks over there are clicking in time with the continental plates shifting. That's going to be a good alert system when another earthquake strikes."

Both Regents turned and saw Gwen, Cantrel, and their daughter Andrielle approaching. And there was Selat, Sulpicett and Bret flying in from the other side.

"Magistrel, we need to talk with you if you don't mind." Gwen's colors never varied, she was so even tempered. Except for now, which surprised Magistrel. He gestured to them and they all flew to a quiet spot where the harvest had left many short clumps of sweet grass still standing.

"Yes, my dear Candela, what brings you here?"

Andrielle spoke first, "It's all my fault, I didn't know what I was doing, and besides, numbers flying around are making me crazy. I've never seen that, and the settling of silk and I don't know what all around my shoulders ..."

"Wait, wait, Andrielle, slow down bit. Gwen? Cantrel?"

Gwen at least looked like she could speak, while Cantrel was intoning the oddest notes. Discordant colors flashed magnesium bright, then toned down and began again a brightening until eyes hurt. "We need some advice because I think our Andrielle here is paired with a Tureg. In fact, that one over there talking with the other Regent."

"What?"

After hearing their story Magistrel told the family to go back to their compartment and that he would send word to them. He flew back to the boulder, and saw that Talandat was alone, the three Tureg he'd been talking with were flying off.

"Well, the time has come, hasn't it?" Magistrel looked resigned. "Now do you believe what I was saying? Andrielle began by telling me in private council that she could sense numbers, and has also finally admitted that she can sense things landing on her shoulders, sometimes a kick or a shove, or a quick caress on her cheek."

"And I've just heard from Bret that he's hearing music, and tasting things. Does Andrielle still taste, and hear music, too?"

"Yes, and Bret continues with Tureg sensations as well?"

"Yes."

Both began thinking. Talandat pacing and Magistrel seated, chin in hand.

Magistrel looked up. "The time has come, dear friend. What we only suspected might eventually happen between our two fey, has actually come to pass. Believe it or not, this is a great new day, and we will grow wiser with this knowledge. But what a shock, not just for us, but for Andrielle and Bret. Wait until they hear."

Talandat answered, "Let's send word to them to gather with the two of us, under the Rosa rugosa shrub this time, and they need to bring their parents with them. This will be tough to explain. The seamless universe has decreed it. There's nothing anyone can do about it."

~ Chapter 20 ~

When the hummingbird brought the message to Andrielle, she began seeing numbers interspersed in the trills of musical notes. Thinking about her mother and father caused a soft milkweed blanket to surround her. Nothing was there, no one could see it, but Andrielle could feel it. How long was this going to go on? The three of them, daughter, mother and father, flew off to the Rosa rugosa shrub, the scene where she had first collided with Bret. That wasn't so long ago.

There they were, Bret and three other Tureg, one of them their Regent.

Bret approached Andrielle and spoke first. "Andrielle, I would like to present to you my mother and father, Sulpicett and Selat of the Tureg fey, and I also wish to present my Regent, Talandat." Andrielle could see numerical equations drifting up from Tureg wings in generous blue-red and orange-green flares. This was all so formal to her.

"Bret, I'd like to present Magistrel, Regent of the Candela fey, and my mother and father, Gwen and Selat."

All four parents started to fly in slow circles around the two young fey. They spun out color after color, their swirls encompassing all of them in synchronous simplicity. The warm hues underscored the cool. Music intoned from Cantrel and Gwen, and numerals streamed from Sulpicett and Selat.

As they all settled down once again, Talandat spoke, "Magistrel and I have been companions for many an eon. From the first, we knew that a time might come when our two fey would evolve. We believe that day has now arrived."

Magistrel continued, "Andrielle of the Candela and Bret of the Tureg, you are the first of the new evolved fey. We shall from this day forward call your fledging community, Nimbus, meaning the circle of light, and we congratulate you. I'm sure that you are wondering what we are talking about, don't you?"

"Yes, sir," Bret looked very serious.

Andrielle was holding her breath, then let out a sigh. "Are you sure you have the right ones? I don't feel any diff ... wait a minute, is this all about the numbers I'm seeing?"

Talandat answered her. "Partly, and haven't you also felt the swirl of your colors landing on your shoulders now and then? Maybe it began when you and Bret first met, maybe that was when he first began to hear music."

The parents of both Andrielle and Bret could not be contained. Bret's father asked a question that must have been on all their minds, "Will they have to leave?"

"That's a real possibility," Magistrel said. "In fact, there may be other fey who are beginning to evolve. Much depends on when and what the seamless universe reveals about the new Nimbus mission. Even if Andrielle and Bret have to leave our caverns and live in one of their own, we are all one family again. And the feud is ended, finally, once and for all. Everyone can now work together."

Talandat smiled as he said, "It looks like this Celebration is a resounding success, to say the least. Andrielle and Bret, your evolved senses put you at the forefront of discovery in the garden. Your missions are yet to be determined, and what they are will help the garden in new ways yet to unfold."

As Magistrel approached Andrielle and Bret, he said, "It's as if the two of you are from the beginning, all over again. What magical times we live in." In his hands was a box made of hardened lava. In each of the many crevices were yellow tendrils. He explained that they were the first sulfur blooms on lava as new land formed in the garden. He told them they should open the box. Bret took it from Magistrel's hands and turned to Andrielle. She lifted the cover and there was glowing warmth, numbers, colors, and music all swirling together. Fragrance wafted out, delicate and sure. They turned to their Regents for an explanation.

Talandat explained, "This is the first fallen star that fey ever captured. Magistrel and I wondered why in the garden or in the name of the seamless universe that all senses were bundled together, since Candela and Tureg always had separate sensations. But we had our suspicions, didn't we, Magistrel?"

"Indeed, and I am very happy that I lived to see Nimbus fey come into existence. I believe the two of you will work in wondrous ways for the good of the garden, the people, and all fey communities."

Talandat turned to Magistrel. "I think, old friend, that tonight's banquet is going to be quite an event."

Gerhardt and Cancret gasped. The Dantorak needed to know right away. Both of them had snuck out of the Tureg cavern, and secreted themselves at the edge of the sweet grass field. They calculated that something monumental was up. Stepping out from the edge of an anemone plant whose fibrous stalks were so dense no one could tell they were hiding there, both flew away under cover of mandrake and woodland poppies. There was a fissure somewhere close by. Just right for dropping a message down to the Dantorak. Wait until they get a load of this!

Colandid nearly tripped as he quickly flew to his quartz crystal. He summoned his council to hear the staggering news: Nimbus had begun. They should have annihilated the worthless humans when they had the chance, way before the seamless universe changed the game and decreed winged fey should evolve. If Colandid had any hair, he'd have pulled it out! Well, there was plenty they could do to see that this so-called Nimbus wouldn't be all sunshine and stars. There was plenty they could do. More sinkholes, more tsunamis, more wildfires. More of everything so heaped on their precious humans, those miserable winged fey won't know which way to turn. There was going to be such a torrent of disasters as to shake the very seamless universe itself. Climate changes were developing, albeit slowly, so now would be a perfect time to step that up. New weather patterns had recently emerged. Devastating drought over larger and larger land masses were already causing havoc. The Dantorak would intensify these trends. The garden was at stake. The beautiful garden, so full of the fruits of the seamless universe, was laid to waste time and again by humans who ignored even the most blatant of warnings. They'll be sorry, they'll be sorry.

The banquet could not have happened under clearer skies. A star shower crackled overhead while juniper and artemisia tonic flowed. Each and every Tureg and Candela household had outdone themselves with an array of succulent dishes prepared for the enjoyment of both fey. Looking down the long tables set with gossamer sculpture and strewn with cornflower and sunflower petals, Andrielle and Bret saw many of their favorite dishes: stews of Mandeville vine buds, hawthorns, with a twist of pokeberry; compotes of wild strawberries, blackberries and hibiscus flowers, seasoned with sweet cicely; sumac cones with dewberry crème, sprinkled with Persian jewel seeds. There was something for everyone. During the feast, each fey community employed rotating crews to patrol the garden so that all fey could partake. Bret hoped the pairing off ceremony was delayed so that he could speak with Jondett first.

He found her standing with Zac, talking in a low murmur. Their numerals were beginning to reflect each other. Mmmm, maybe this wouldn't be so hard to explain after all.

He was wrong.

As soon as Jondett saw him approach, a magnesium blast from her fist collided with his chin and he went catapulting backwards into the brush.

"How dare you? How could you? You were lying to me all this time?"

"Now wait, Jondett, let me explain, I ... I didn't ..."

"Forget it! I reject the invitation to pair with you for all time. You taking care of me? That's a laugh—you're rejected. Your plea for synchronicity—rejected." With that, Jondett slumped into the waiting arms of Zac who smirked at Bret.

Bret stood up, and said, "I only wish you well, Jondett, you and Zac. He is a good fey, and your pairing will ... enhance the ... seamless universe." He turned away, as it was impossible to explain what he could not understand himself.

Andrielle stood waiting, looking askance at him. He wondered if she had as many misgivings about all this as he did. The expression on her face conveyed unmistakable uncertainty. Perhaps the seamless universe didn't know what it was doing. Was that even a possibility? It was just so hard to imagine that the old ways were gone and the future would bring something new and different. How could the old ways be gone? Hadn't they worked for time immemorial? All of his beliefs, and no doubt hers, were about to be converted into so much mist, and through that veil, there was no telling what was waiting. Bret took Andrielle by the hand and they went forward to the waiting feast.

Acknowledgements:

Since a young girl, I've relished mythology and fairy tales, those classic fantastic concoctions of brilliant minds. Roman, Greek, and Norse mythology, Grimm's *Fairy Tales* and Hans Christian Andersen books hid under my pillow to be read by flashlight. Then I discovered C.S. Lewis' *Chronicles of Narnia*, J. R. R. Tolkien's *Trilogy* and *Silmarillion*, and Cervantes' *Don Quixote*. The worlds these authors created were places I longed to live in, if only it were possible.

Fascinated with writing long fiction, thanks in part to conducting workshops on writing novels, I wrote, too. It felt good to walk the walk, not just talk about it. Ever since, I've been engrossed in my fantasy world and characters, as is the way of the seamless universe. My thanks to Schoolcraft College, and the staff of the MacGuffin for teaching and speaking opportunities.

With deep appreciation to my readers without whose help and inspiration I could not have accomplished this novel: my spouse Victor for his stalwart support; my writing friends Annemarie Pedersen, Linda Fletcher, Sue Glover, Perry Zimmerman, Mike Nichoff, Kevin O'Connor, Jerry Birdsall, Don Beyer, Robin Franks, Lorene and

Robert Erickson, Arthur Lindenberg, Steve Dolgin, members of Detroit Working Writers and Associated Writing Programs; animated readers and friends Diane Pittaway, Loretta and Joe Lang, Deb and Ed Swain, Donna and Steve Pezda, Martha Phillips, Donna and Jim Nawrot, Karen and Charlie Smith, Bea and Mike Gravino, Ernest Porcari, Claudia Capos, Doug Taylor, Ardis McLeod; and my dear family members who provide never ending love, support and encouragement: Carollynne, Larry, Eric, Patrick and Christopher Kelly, Robert Ripley, Joseph W. Leo, Marilyn and Joseph J. Leo, Mark, Susie, Owen and Isaiah Leo.

Today, may something seamless in the universe happen to you, too.

Kathleen Ripley Leo, award-winning poet/novelist, lives in Northville, Michigan, with her husband Victor, a glass artist. She is the author of eight volumes of poems and editor of poetry/fiction anthologies. She received two Special Tributes from the Michigan Legislature for her work as a Creative Writer in the Schools made possible thru grants from National Endowment for the Arts and Michigan Council for the Arts. She was commissioned by the city of Northville and the Michigan Council for the Arts to write a book of poems chronicling the history of their city for the Michigan Sesquicentennial, entitled **Town One South**. She is a member of the American Academy of Poets, Association of Writers and Writing Programs, Detroit Working Writers, and listed in Poets and Writers Directory. Countless people have taken her classes, seminars and workshops in creative writing at Schoolcraft College, and at national conferences.

31108326R00125

Made in the USA
Charleston, SC
06 July 2014